The Rio Verde Series

Book Two

I0630723

Fresh Faith

By

Elise Phillips

The Rio Verde Series

Book One: Restoration Road
Book Two: Fresh Faith
Book Three: Healing Hope

Dedication

For Amanda and Melanie
who taught me that church friends
are some of the very best kinds of friends.

Table of Contents

Chapter One

"Oh you have got to be kidding me."

"No, Miss Abbott, I am not. You have inherited a bakery. Now let's discuss the terms of your grandfather's will."

"Can I have a minute? I need to process this."

The stiff and formal man smiled at me, kindness radiating out from him. John Coulter. I'd just met him but he appeared to be a stand-up kind of guy. Perfectly sane and all that. Not someone who'd make up wild stories. He had to be making up what he'd just told me though. There was no way it was real.

"This is crazy."

"It's what Harry wanted. He left a video too. He knew you wouldn't believe the will alone."

Harry. My grandfather. I had never met him. Never even seen a picture of him. Clearly he'd kept tabs on me though and had some sort of love for me to have left me his bakery. It was all so surreal though.

I started to protest but John turned his laptop around to face me, a video of my grandfather appearing on the screen. His bald head shined in the sunlight streaming in through an unseen window on his left. I looked around and realized I was sitting in the same spot he'd been in, the same window was casting a square of light over my head, the same collection of paintings populated by flying ducks and armed men in camouflage hung behind us both.

"Is this thing running, Johnny?" His voice was rough, each word clipped and short. He glared at the camera, grumpy at the world. For some reason that didn't surprise me at all. The very few times my mom had told me about her father she had made him sound like a difficult man, a cruel man. Grumpy fit more with the man I was seeing. Not awful, just gruff and surly. As he and John grumbled back and forth on screen I just stared. He was a stranger to me. His craggy

1

face. His mouth framed with deep creases. He looked worn out by life. His eyes though -- bright green and clear. Those were familiar. Those were my mom's eyes. Those were my eyes. With a bit of familiarity to anchor me, I caught more similarities. The dent on the bridge of his nose. The little gap between his top two front teeth. I saw the same features in my own face each time I looked in a mirror. I wondered if he'd once had red hair too or if Mom and I had gotten that from my grandmother.

"Now you listen here, Joy Claire Abbott. I'm some of the only family you've got left and I'm dying." He paused, coughing -- a deep, ugly sound which made me wince. "Your mom took off with you when you were just a baby so I know you don't know who I am. I've tried to keep track of you both. I know she lost you when she got lost herself. I know you've also made a name for yourself as a better-than-average baker. If you're watching this, I've kicked it so now is your chance. This bakery has been in our family since it was built. It's yours now, but you've got to work for it. I want you to stay here, in Rio Verde, for a year. Run the shop. You know how, Abbotts have been baking for generations. It's in your DNA. So for a year you stay put. You run the shop. You make a go of it. After the year is up you can sell it if you want. For a year though you're going to try to do what your mother never could. Stay put and give this place a chance."

He started to cough again, going white. Mr. Coulter appeared on the edge of the frame, handing him a bottle of water. Harry drank and composed himself again.

"Get yourself to church too, girl. That is part of the terms as well. Write it down, Johnny. I want the girl to get to know the Lord."

The video froze and John turned the laptop back around, closing it. "There you have it, from the man himself."

"Is all of this really legal?" It was the only thing I could think to ask. My mind was full of questions. Questions I knew full well the gray-haired lawyer couldn't even begin to answer for me.

"It is. The estate was his. He could put any terms on it he wanted to. I've seen stranger demands."

2

I leaned back in the chair, the leather squeaking as I moved. For a while I just sat and thought. I couldn't believe the luck. Things like this never happened to me. I didn't trust it, but I was curious enough to want to know more.

"So what does all this mean?" I finally asked.

Mr. Coulter rested his arms on the desk, sliding the will toward me. "I think you know, Miss Abbott."

"I'm home and the newest owner of Abbott Bakery?"

"Looks like it."

A voice inside me whispered to just get up and leave. It was a familiar voice. It had kept me moving around, wandering the country, since I was eighteen. I took the will, laying it in the empty chair beside me. There didn't appear to be any way out of this -- at least not a way that I wanted to take. Of course I could just refuse the inheritance. I didn't want to though. In the past week I'd run out of options. Lost my job. Got evicted out of my apartment. I had maybe a grand in my bank account and everything I owned had fit into my old Bronco SUV a little too easily. I could go to Las Vegas, see if Mom was still living there. Staying here and running a bakery was probably much less likely to end in a fight or tears. It might be nice to have something steady for once. Something I wasn't renting or borrowing from someone else. It would be nice to have a safety net. I'd never had one of those.

"So what's the next step?"

"Let's head over to the bakery and discuss it. You'll need to see the condition of things in person. I'll just call Will and have him meet us there."

"Call who?"

"Will. Will Bell. He's the executor of your grandfather's estate."

"You mean you're not..."

"Oh goodness no. I'm not a money guy. Will took over Harry's finances a while back. He's great with numbers. From here on out you'll work with him. He'll handle the bakery's finances until your year is up and you assume ownership of everything."

As he picked up the phone, I grabbed the will and moved to see myself out. Mr. Coulter whispered to meet them at the bakery when I stood. I nodded in agreement then escaped the office, fleeing to the street below. From the front doors of the law office I could see Abbott Bakery. It sat on one corner of the city square. The center of the city. Beside it a hardware store the was the Rio Verde bank building. A quick forty-five degree turn and another block of businesses. Then another and another. The square of businesses circled a grassy park crowned by a stone gazebo. The park held several huge trees, the leaves just starting to turn towards their fall colors. Everything looked old in this square. No, historic. It all looked like it had been here for generations. I turned back to the bakery. Two stories of deep red brick, it was a narrow building. The Rio Verde Bank took up the majority of the block, leaving just a sliver on one end for the bakery and the hardware store.

I walked closer, appraising the building as I crossed the street. The second floor was full of tall windows, each crowned with a white rectangle of stone. The white and red was a contrast I loved. I pictured a bright, open loft inside and hoped I was right. Over the front door on a white lintel stone was the date 1910. Over one hundred years old. From the outside it looked like it was still in good shape. The windows flanking the front door had sheets of plywood nailed over them and a closed for business sign was taped to the door itself. Goodness knows what was waiting for me inside. I stepped backward off the curb, look up at the front of the bakery. If it was possible, the place looked sad and a little lost. Both things I understood well. I hoped that for once, staying in one place for longer than six months wouldn't bite me in the butt. I hoped maybe, just maybe, I had finally found home.

Chapter Two

"Oh goodnight, it's hot in here." I stopped just a few steps into the shop, a wall of heat halting my steps.

Coulter walked through the door behind me, flipping a switch and flooding the bakery with light. It was a wreck but it could have been worse. It just looked dirty and messy but nothing seemed to be broken down. Tables were scattered around the front of the store, all covered with old sheets. The random patterns on the fabric -- flowers and stripes and even tiny cartoon kittens -- were hidden under a layer of fine dust. Along the wall Abbott's shared with the business next door was a display case and a stack of chairs in a corner. The chairs and the floor wore the same coating of dirty brown powdery dust. I glanced down the long hallway, seeing a side door and stairs leading up to the apartment above. More fine dust. Under all the dust and clutter though it was beautiful.

Wide plank wood floors I hoped were original to the building. Two big glass fronted display cases, making an L-shaped half wall before the swinging doors and the kitchen. An old black cash register stood alone on the counter like a sentry. I wanted to pull the plywood off the windows and see the place in the sunlight. I wanted to roll up my sleeves and make the place my own.

"I'll go turn on the AC." He slipped through the opening between the display cases, entering the kitchen. I was on his heels, eager to see what was always my favorite spot in any bakery. When he turned on the lights I froze.

"Whoa."

"Harry modernized the kitchen two years ago." Coulter spoke as he crossed the kitchen to the controls for the air conditioning. Soon a welcome hum filled the room, followed by a wave of cool air. The trees in the square outside might be getting ready for fall but summer hadn't quite left Texas yet. The AC brought a welcome cool breeze into the stuffy shop.

"I'd say so." I walked through the kitchen in shock. The front of the shop didn't look as though it had changed since the bakery opened back in 1910. The kitchen though -- it was amazing. Everything was stainless steel and lustrous even under the coating of dust. There was a new, massive gas stove and four new ovens, two big and two small. There was a long, marble workstation in the center of the room, perfect for everything from making candy to kneading dough. Right next to the ovens were sleek, new cooling racks for everything from bread to cookies. Past the huge commercial fridge was a walk in freezer. Around a corner by the door to the loading dock was a big storage area full of shelves just waiting for all the necessary staples to run the bakery. It was waiting for someone to take over -- waiting for me.

We both jumped when a crash echoed down from the second floor.

"What was that?"

"Probably the cat."

It wasn't Coulter who answered me. I turned around to see another stranger walking into the kitchen from the side entrance off the hall. This must be the money guy Will Bell. I hadn't heard him come into the bakery behind us. I'd been too consumed with the overwhelming beauty of the kitchen. We locked eyes for a brief second and I quickly looked away from him, a single butterfly coming to life in my stomach, fluttering a moment before I forced it to be still.

"There's a cat?" Coulter looked up toward the ceiling, confusion on his face.

"Yeah. I saw signs of one upstairs the last time I checked on the place."

Pushing past both men, I headed out to the side hallway and turned toward the stairs. Will had turned on the hall light and I could see the first floor's layer of dust carried on up to the second floor. I was going to need a hazmat suit to clean this place. The dust would be overwhelming once I started to vacuum.

At the top of the stairs I wasn't surprised to see the door pushed open. Any cat I'd ever known had been able to open doors. If one had moved into the bakery it had probably made itself very much at home, patrolled both floors, hunting and guarding the home it had claimed. Stepping inside, I paused to turn on the lights and take it all in. In an instant I was dizzy. Overwhelmed. Standing in a place that had been home to generations of my family was almost too much to handle. All those years of life -- the decades of laughter, tears, sadness, anger -- it all swept over me. I tried to picture Mom as a little girl, living here. I couldn't do it. I couldn't picture her as anything more than the mess she'd been my whole life.

Taking a deep breath, I stepped inside, the guys still a few paces behind, their twin footsteps marking their progress on the narrow staircase. I jumped when Will touched me then pointed over my shoulder. His touch made me focus on the here and now and I was dizzy again, this time overwhelmed by the state of the place.

"You'll have to get some work done before you can move in to the apartment I'm afraid."

"What happened?" I stepped away from them, trying to take in the ruins of what had been the apartment's kitchen and dining room.

"We had some big storms over the summer. Lightning hit the building." Will walked past me and pointed up. There were sheets of plywood and plastic tarps where the ceiling should have been. Now I knew how the cat had gotten in.

I made myself look away from the ruined ceiling and Will, focusing on the rest of my new home. Before me was a half wall surrounding the kitchen. Well, what had been the kitchen. Everything in the horseshoe shaped room was broken and warped from a combination of fire and water damage. The exterior wall where a ruined range hood and the skeletal remains of cabinets hung was covered in a blanket of thick ash. The cabinet frames stood open, the doors burnt away or lying on the floor.

"You got lucky. Some of the Sheriff's Department guys were close by. They called the fire department and the fire was put out pretty fast. It could have been a lot worse. My cousin is a contractor. A house she was restoring got hit by lightning too, they lost a brand new roof and part of the second floor."

I turned away from the ruins of the kitchen, looking over the rest of the space, heaving a sigh of relief when I realized the damage had been contained to the kitchen.

"Are you sure nothing else was damaged?"

"Nope. There might be a little water damage on the floors near the kitchen but it was all contained to here. I've already got Mallie on the line for you. She can start working on it right away. You should be able to move in here in a month or so." I turned my back on both men, thinking of my truck on the street. Everything I owned was in it. Hole in the roof or not, I'd have to move in today. I walked slowly, further into the apartment, still trying to decide if I was really going to stick it out. Aside from the ruined kitchen it was fine. Empty and dirty but fine.

I walked over to one of the wide, tall windows across the front of the apartment. From the spot I had a great view of the square and big gazebo in the center. Opposite the bakery, on the other side of the square, sat The Red, White, and Blue Diner. It was early for dinner but the diner still had a few people inside.

"There's my cousin Mallie down there." Will appeared beside me, pointing down to the sidewalk outside of the diner. A tall blond appeared, pausing to unbuckle a tool belt from her waist then returning to an older pickup. She tossed the belt inside and turned back to the diner.

"That's her fiancé Tres. His family owns The RWB." As he spoke the blond hugged a tall man in a baseball cap. The pair exchanged a quick kiss and went inside arm-in-arm. I smiled. This place was like the set of a feel-good movie. I pivoted away from the window, looking back toward the apartment. I glanced over at Will, letting myself study him as he watched the city from the window. I

8

would have had to be blind to not see how handsome he was. Coffee colored skin and soft, cocoa brown eyes. The suit, the bow tie, the wire frame glasses -- it made for a very good looking nerd. The whole package made the butterfly in my stomach perk back up. *He is not my type.* When Will caught me watching I walked away, ducking into one of the tiny bedrooms. Empty, just like the rest of the place. I wandered into the little Jack and Jill bathroom and into another tiny bedroom. Exiting it, I turned into the master bedroom, happy to see it had an outside wall with a big window in it. The other two bedrooms had felt like caves.

"Where is all the furniture?"

"Harry wanted it sold off. He wanted you to have a fresh start here. None of the old junk he and Nancy had collected." Will walked past me to a side room Mr. Coulter had just opened. I followed him, looking inside. There was a washer, dryer, and a back door. They were all almost buried by a whole lot of boxes.

"Anything family related we boxed up to save for you. Photo albums, some vintage clothes my mom wouldn't let us sell, those sort of things."

"Thank you."

Will smiled and the butterfly in my stomach did a summersault. "I figured you'd like to get to know your grandparents a little."

To my surprise tears flooded my eyes. I turned away, rushing back downstairs, trying to regain control of my emotions. I blamed the past few days on my uncharacteristic mushiness. I was normally so level and even. Having your world fall apart in less than a week would wreck anyone.

I paced around the big kitchen, taking in the white and stainless steel landscape again. This was my world. My kitchen. My bakery. As the words formed in my mind I realized I'd decided to stay. I stopped, glancing around again, stopping in surprise when I spotted a big black and white cat watching me from on top of a cabinet.

"What do you think, kitten? Want to run a bakery with me?" It meowed at me then dashed away as Will and Mr. Coulter walked into the room.

"So what do I need to do to get her running again?"

"I'll leave you two to work out the details." Mr. Coulter came over and shook my hand. "Good to have you here, Joy. Rio Verde hasn't been the same without an Abbott baking for everyone."

Will walked over to the marble topped island, pulling up a tall stool and laying out a stack of papers. "Let's talk business."

"Just give me a list. I can do it on my own."

"Nope." He tugged a piece a paper free from the top of the stack, holding it out to me. "What does it say?"

I rolled my eyes and sighed and read it out loud. "Let Will help you, Joy Claire."

"Wise man, your grandfather."

I drug a second stool over and smiled despite my irritation. I wouldn't be on my own this time. My grandfather had made sure of it. I wasn't sure I knew how to handle this new world but I was game to try.

"Okay fine, talk to me, Numbers Guy."

Chapter Three

It only took an hour to get things moving forward with the bakery. When I'd gotten the letter from Mr. Coulter a week earlier I'd called him right away, just like the letter had requested. Once I'd touched base with him and let him know when I'd make it to Texas he'd gotten busy. Well, he'd had Will get busy. While I was driving cross-country, questioning my sanity, Will had been working hard. Power and water were already turned on. Phone service had been started. He had even had Internet service hooked up for me. He and Mr. Coulter had planned on me staying. They'd set up everything. Will quickly gave me a list of all the vendors Harry had used and I called them while he activated a bakery credit card for me and wrote down all of the banking information I'd need. He also gave me a personal card connected to a separate account for personal, non-bakery items. He gave me his crisp, white business card before he left, making me promise to call him if I needed any help.

As soon as he was gone I went back out into the still hot September evening and started carrying all of my worldly possessions from the Bronco into the bakery. I stacked everything inside the side door of the shop rather than lug it all upstairs. I was going to need to do a major cleaning up in the apartment before I could unpack and get settled. Plus I'd need important things like furniture. After Will had left, I'd peeked into the bakery office. If I moved the chairs out of the little room there would be enough room to spread out my sleeping bag. Not ideal, but I'd had less fancy accommodations than this before and the office was a lot cleaner than any part of the apartment was.

When the last box was inside I wandered back to the front of the shop, standing in the beam of late day sunlight coming through the open front door. As I let myself relax everything hit me all at once. In the past eight days I'd become homeless, lost my job, found out my grandfather had died, and become the owner of a bakery. I dropped down to the floor, leaning back on my hands to stare at the empty bakery. The cat appeared from nowhere, giving me a cautious meow from beneath a nearby table.

"Come on over, kitten." I patted my lap and it strolled over, carefully sniffing me before climbing into my lap. Soon its purr was filling the quiet. "I guess I should add that I've gotten a cat to my list. It's been a hell of a ride for just over a week." I worked my hands into its soft fur, the volume of its purr going up. I relaxed, closing my eyes as exhaustion washed over me. I was beat. Will had given me a to-do list a mile long. I had to meet with his contractor cousin tomorrow morning. I needed to go over my grandfather's old menu and see if I wanted to bake and sell the same things he had. Will had implied it would be expected for me to stick with it and honor tradition. Which of course made me want to ignore it and do my own thing. I also needed to clean up things down here and at least one bedroom upstairs. Then go buy something to sleep on and groceries for me. The cat flipped over on his back in my lap and I added cat food to the grocery list. All I really wanted to do though was curl up right in the sunbeam and sleep.

"Looks like you've got a big job in front of you."

I jumped out of my skin at the unexpected voice. The cat hissed and shot off into the back of the shop, scaring me almost as much as the sudden visitor.

"Woah. I'm sorry I didn't mean to scare either of you. I just saw you working and thought you could use something to eat." The woman gestured to the brown paper bag she was holding. It bore the logo of The Red, White, and Blue Diner. Then the smell hit me. A burger and fries.

"Bless you. I'm starving." I stood, dusting off my jeans and smiling at the woman before me. Hispanic and tall, I assumed she was from the diner across the square. I wondered if she was a sister of the man engaged to Will's cousin. "I'm Joy. Joy Abbott." I held out my hand, laughing when she handed me the bag of food instead of shaking my hand.

"Sorry. Full hands." She held out a drink too. I took it, immediately taking a long drink. "I'm Luz Baca. My family owns The RWB. You come over anytime you need something to eat. Or anything else. We're all happy to have the bakery opening up again. Everyone has missed it."

Before I could say anything else she turned to go, saying she had to get back to work. I took my dinner to the bench in front of the bakery, watching her cross the square and return to work, wondering how she'd known I would need something to eat. As she walked inside someone handed her a little kid. As Luz shifted the child onto her hip, smiling and kissing the mop of dark hair that crowned its head I realized how she'd known. She was a mom. Moms always knew when someone was hungry. Well, moms other than my own. She'd never had those kinds of instincts. I'd had foster mothers who had had that sixth sense though, always knowing when I'd come home hungry or sad or angry. Looks like Luz had it too.

As I dug into the burger and fries I watched the city wind down for the day. Business at the diner picked up as people stopped by for supper on their way home. The ice cream shop diagonal from the bakery also saw an increase in business, many people walking over from The RWB after eating. The other restaurants in the center of the city were busy too. Other places -- stores, the pharmacy -- shut down for the day, lights going out and owners or managers walking out the front door and locking up.

It had been a while since I'd lived in a town this small. It was so different from the larger cities I'd been calling a temporary home. Here business owners stopped to visit with people walking by. Cars paused in the middle of the street as the drivers rolled down their windows to visit for a moment. Diners walked around the square after eating instead of jumping in their cars and speeding away. Everything was slowed down here. When the sun started to dip below the buildings around the square I forced myself to get up and go inside the shop. I locked up the front door and headed to the stack of boxes I'd left in the hallway. I dug through them until I found my sleeping bag, then headed to the office. I needed to turn it into a bedroom before I fell asleep on my feet. The cat trotted before me, bounding into the worn, threadbare office chair and settling in to supervise my work.

Chapter Four

I walked across the square the next morning, hoping breakfast from The Red, White, and Blue Diner would be as good as the burger Luz had brought me the night before. It turned out to be as cute a place inside as it was outside. All bright colors and chrome. Stools along the long counter, big booths along the windows. I remembered a similar place from my childhood. Mom had worked there during one of her good stretches. I had walked there each day after school, claiming a stool beside the register, doing homework and reading until closing. I remembered Mom in the yellow and white apron laughing and joking with the customers, calling them *Honey* and *Sugar* while she brought them food. I'd seen hundreds of diners like it in the years since those days. All a piece of the past, time capsules of life before cell phones, the internet, and distrust for strangers. I sought them out, trying to hang on to my own time capsule, trying to hold on to that brief slice of goodness in my childhood.

I pulled myself back to the present as a waitress passed my way. I smiled when I saw it was Luz. She carried a food-laden tray with one hand and balanced a smiling toddler on the opposite hip. She moved with an unhurried grace.

"Welcome to The Red, White, and Blue, Joy" she said as she paused before me. "Sit wherever you like. I'll run over a menu in just a sec."

I claimed one of the red bar stools as another customer came through the door. At the sound of the door chime Luz headed for the woman, handing off the baby with just a smile. The new arrival grinned ear to ear at the baby girl. I recognized her as Will's cousin and my future contractor.

"How's my girl doing today?" She cradled the child with care and claimed a stool just down from my own.

"She'd like a sleepover at her aunt's house. Very much."

"She wearing y'all out?"

"Two weeks of no sleep, Mallie Jo. I think she's trying to kill us."

"Well..."

"Did I mention how much she has missed you?"

The blond just smiled down at the baby then kissed her forehead. "I'd be happy to take her tonight, Luz. My dad may kill me, but I bet little Ria will win him over."

Luz sighed with obvious relief. "Bless you. Teo and I are exhausted." She slipped behind the counter and passed me a menu before returning to Mallie.

"Why are you here for breakfast? Shouldn't you be headed to a job site somewhere? I thought y'all were working out of town right now."

"Dad is. He's finishing up the Tillman house north of town. I'm starting a new job. Will got it lined up for me. I'll be across the street at the bakery for the next while."

"Oh. Then you'll be working for Joy."

"Who's Joy?" I smiled when Luz looked over to me. Mallie copied her movement, confusion on her face.

"That'd be me." I slipped off my stool and walked over to her, holding out my hand. "I'm Joy Abbott. New owner of Abbott's Bakery."

She stared at my hand for several seconds before her friend reached across the counter and poked her in the shoulder. Then she took my hand and grinned at me.

"Mallory Andrews. One half of Andrews and Andrews Restoration."

"Glad to meet you. Let me treat you to breakfast before you come see my wreck."

"A wreck? Mallie loves a wreck. You should have seen my brother's house before she and her dad restored it. It was a dump but they turned it into a stunner." Luz leaned her elbows on the counter,

16

looking from Mallie to me with a smile, enjoying bragging on her friend.

"Luz!"

All three of us jumped and looked toward the kitchen at the sudden and gruff voice. An older man scowled through the opening at her.

"Oh! Sorry, Dad." Luz pushed herself away from the counter, stepping back into her working persona. "I'm sorry, what can I get y'all for breakfast?"

We both ordered and Luz vanished into the kitchen then returned with a tray of food, taking care of other customers. I turned back toward Mallie, asking, "Why do you like wrecks?"

"Oh, Mallie saves houses." Luz put a plate before me, the mouth watering aroma of the small stack of pancakes set my stomach grumbling. While I ate, Mallory gave me a quick explanation of how she'd come to run a business with her father. They focused on saving and restoring old houses, places other people would have torn down. I was surprised when she told me the first house they'd saved had belonged to the man who was about to become her husband.

"It was a God thing," she stated simply.

"A God thing?" I couldn't help but ask. Normally I steered clear of any mention of faith and God but her certainty was intriguing.

"Oh yeah, a God thing. When everything you thought was going wrong comes together into something almost perfectly right and you can look back and see God's hand in every winding step that led you to the spot He wanted you to be at. A God thing."

Luz appeared beside her, reclaiming the now sleeping baby. "She's right. It was a God thing. If things hadn't gone wrong in her life and derailed her dreams she wouldn't have ended up moving home. If things hadn't gone wrong in my brother's life, he wouldn't have come home and bought the farm and found the house everyone had forgotten. If the housing boom hadn't tanked, Mallie's dad wouldn't have been looking for new projects. God did it all to bring them together to save the house and to put Mallie and Tres together so they could fall in love."

She tucked the baby against her shoulder and gave Mallory a quick, one-armed hug. "I'm going to run her over to Mom's now that Marisol is here." As she spoke a younger version of her appeared behind the counter. The younger sister she'd mentioned.

"I'll swing over and steal her when I'm done for the day. You and Teo enjoy your night off. Love you, Lucy Lou."

"Love you too, Mallie Jo. Good seeing you again, Joy."

I was thrown off by the exchange between the two friends. I'd never had a friend who was so affectionate. The 'L' word wasn't something I had heard much in my life and yet here were two friends tossing it around without a thought. I was starting to feel better and better about getting suckered into moving to this little town. It was a special place.

"So."

"So what," I said to Mallory as she reached over the counter and grabbed a nearby pot of coffee.

"Tell me about this wreck of yours," she said with a grin.

Chapter Five

"You know, I always wanted to come up here when I was a kid. I thought living over a bakery would be so cool."

I pushed open the door and let Mallie go into the apartment first. "This will be a first for me. I've never had the chance to renovate something."

"You'll have fun with it, trust me. You'll get the chance to make it your own. Maybe you'll get to know your grandparents a bit too since you never lived here or knew them."

"How'd you know that?"

"Will. Mr. Coulter wouldn't tell me anything but Will filled me in."

"Nosey much?" I smirked at her, not minding at all that she'd grilled Will on me. Normally that sort of prying would get to me but for some reason, from her it didn't.

She laughed at my question. "Hey, it's a small town. I've got to find entertainment somehow."

I couldn't help but laugh. Small town life was going to take some getting used to. "No. I never lived here. I was born here but my mom took off with me when I was still a baby."

"Well you didn't miss out on much. Rio Verde was a quiet place to grow up. Your grandparents though, they were cool. I was always hanging out over at The RWB so I'd come over here for cookies all the time. They'd always give me more than I paid for."

She stopped hard as she came around the corner, staring at the ruins of my kitchen. "Woah. You weren't kidding. This is a total gut."

I hung back, watching her as she worked her way through the rubble. She was totally at ease in the mess. Tool belt hung around her waist, pad and pencil in hand, she gracefully worked her way through the broken cabinets and piles of junk, making notes. She stopped, using one of the still standing lower cabinets as a desk, sketching something out on her pad.

"Okay, so here's what I'm thinking." At her declaration I joined her among the ruins to see her drawing of my new kitchen. The page held a collection of rough squares and rectangles. It made zero sense to me.

"You're going to have to give me some direction here, Mallie. I see geometry, not a kitchen."

She laughed and pulled the yellow legal pad back toward her, giving it a spin as she faced it back her way then adding labels to it.

"Here." This time she did more than slide the pad over to me. She leaned over and pointed out everything, explaining as she went along. As she spoke the squares and rectangles took form. I saw two big islands instead of the half wall currently blocking the kitchen off from the bedrooms. The short end of the kitchen that had held what I guessed was once a pantry was gone too, turning the kitchen from a blocked in U to an open, galley style space.

"It's perfect, Mallie. Nice and open. It looks like this was a dead end kind of a kitchen. Your version is so much better."

"Awesome. I'll measure and get you a proper estimate written up. Any color or style preferences you want me to keep in mind?"

"I... I don't know. I've never thought about that kind of stuff. I've never had a proper, big kitchen of my own."

"Not even in rent houses or apartments?"

I laughed a sad sort of laugh and explained how I'd spent most of my adult life renting single rooms instead of houses or apartments. Sometimes there wasn't even a room to call mine, just a couch to sleep on. "Even when I was a kid it was like that. Mom and I bounced around a lot."

She regarded me for a moment or two, letting my words sink in. I guessed she was imagining the gypsy-like life I'd led. She narrowed her eyes like she was thinking up some sort of plan, tilting her head as she continued to stare at me.

Trying to distract her, I pointed toward the rooms along the interior wall that was my shared border with the bank next door. "Those rooms over there are total caves. No windows, no natural light. Do you think you could do something about them while you're rebuilding my kitchen?"

"We could maybe put some skylights in," she said, crossing the narrow apartment to peer into the two bedrooms. "One in the bathroom too. Maybe add a transom -- a narrow window -- over all the doors. It would be more in keeping with the age of the building. Then give the rooms a fresh coat of paint. They'd be like brand new rooms without all the work of a total renovation."

I looked into one of the rooms, staring up toward the ceiling. The idea of sunlight streaming into each room sounded wonderful. Windows would have been better but I couldn't exactly scoot the bakery over and create an alley between it and the hardware store next door.

"Can you do that and give me a new kitchen before your wedding?"

She turned, looking confused.

"Will told me."

A smile lit up her face when she looked at the simple diamond ring on her finger. "He has such a big mouth. I've got plenty of time before the wedding, so don't you worry." She pulled the tape measure off her belt and starting measuring the kitchen, making notes on her pad.

"Where are you going to live while we get the apartment in shape?" She tossed the question at me as she measured the doorway of one of the little bedrooms.

"Over there," I said, pointed at the master bedroom.

"Are you sure? It's going to be a wreck around here."

"You must have missed the stack of boxes in the hall. I haven't got any place to go. I crashed in the office last night but I'm going to clean up the bedroom today and go buy an air mattress or something.

It'll be dusty but it will be better than a sleeping bag on a very hard floor."

She narrowed her eyes again, staring at me, her sky blue eyes intense.

"You've got to stop with the intense stare, Mallie," I said, breaking her laser-like gaze.

"Sorry." She smiled and tapped her temple. "I know someone who can help you. Luz's sister Isabel is a decorating whiz. I'll send her by today. You need more than an air mattress. You've got a whole apartment to furnish." She tucked her tape measure back on her belt with a flourish and grinned at me.

Chapter Six

As soon as Mallie was gone I attacked the first floor. Or I attempted to attack the first floor. I tried to start with the boarded up windows but couldn't tug them free with my bare hands and couldn't find any sort of tools anywhere in the bakery. I kicked myself for not asking Mallie to pull the plywood off for me. I turned my attention to the collection of tables and chairs in the front of the shop next, pulling off all the sheets only to create a dust storm that filled the entire first floor with a choking brown fog. After opening the front door, side door, and the big door on the loading dock at the back of the kitchen to clear out the dust I turned to the closet under the stairs, deciding to get rid of the massive dirt problem before moving forward with any other cleaning projects. After dragging out boxes of Christmas decorations, Thanksgiving decorations, Halloween decorations, and more I found an ancient mop and broom in the back of the closet. The rope strings of the mop stuck to the floor when I picked it up. Bristles from the broom did the same with more cascading from the head as I lifted it. With a sigh I tossed them both in the dumpster in the alley and closed up the shop. I grabbed my spanking new business credit card and headed to the big Walmart I'd seen on the edge of town.

I was pushing my stuffed-to-the-gills cart through the sheets and towels section when she found me.

"Hi, kiddo."

I froze at the familiar voice. I shook my head no, my stomach sinking like a cannonball as I turned to face her.

"Mom?"

She looked the same. Almost the same at least. She looked more like me now. Or I looked more like her. Same red hair. Same fair skin. Same bridge of freckles across the same nose. She wore more wrinkles around her eyes and mouth than I did, but she still looked mostly the same.

Her sameness made me furious. I felt my expression shift from shock to anger, felt my face warm with emotion. Everything around us faded into the background. The other shoppers. The store employees. The 1980's music playing throughout the store. I narrowed my eyes and started to shake my head again. This wasn't real. This couldn't be happening.

"No. No. No. You are not going to walk up to me in Walmart like you saw me yesterday. No." I turned away quickly and grabbed my wallet from the shopping cart, walking away from her, my groceries and cleaning supplies forgotten.

I heard her call my name and start to follow me so I ducked down a random aisle. When she followed I turned down a second one and then a third. Suddenly it hit me that I was running from my mother in Walmart.

In fact I was on the verge of flat out sprinting away from her. Thirty-one years old and I was running from my mom like an out of control toddler. I stopped my retreat and made myself turn and face her. Out of the corner of my eye I realized we were about to have a standoff in the toilet paper aisle. It was somehow very fitting. I was almost certain everything she was going to tell me was going to be total crap.

Then there she was. She stopped, surprised to find me waiting for her. I watched, waiting for her to get close enough to hear me.

"What are you doing here, Mom?"

"You've grown up, Joy Claire."

"That's what happens when you vanish from your child's life for close to two decades."

She flinched and looked at the floor, shame coloring her face. I felt like a bad person but I was glad my words had hurt her. I would have welcomed her back into my life if it had just been a year. Or even two. She'd passed the line of forgiveness a long time ago. It was petty and childish and I didn't care. I wanted to hurt her as much as she'd hurt me.

She dug through her purse and pulled out a big envelope, holding it out toward me. For a moment I was confused then I saw the return address. Coulter and Dixon.

"You got a letter too?"

"I did."

I turned away, taking a few steps then circling back to her. I didn't understand this. How had John Coulter managed to get a letter to my mom when I'd been trying to find her for over a decade? *No, I reminded myself, not quite. I gave up looking several years back.*

Finally, I met her eyes, angry when tears started to flood my vision. "Where have you been? I... I looked for you for so long." I turned away again, looking up at the ceiling far above us before returning my eyes to a spot just past her left shoulder. I made myself focus on the labels on the massive packages of toilet paper as I tried to get control of my emotions. Around us people kept on shopping, oblivious to the storm of emotions building between my mom and me. I'd imagined confronting her dozens of times but never had I thought it would happen in a grocery store. Never thought it would have a soundtrack of aggressively cheerful music either.

The storm inside of me built up as I stared just past her. I struggled to hold onto myself. I had thought I was over all of this. I was realizing no amount of years, no amount of work on myself was going to get rid of the kid inside of me who wanted her mom to come home and love her.

"I got kind of lost for a while." She repeated my own unconscious gesture -- looking to the ceiling to pause and gather herself. "I got very, very lost. I just wasn't any good for you, Joy. I was screwing up our life. I didn't want you to end up like me. A high school dropout. A single mom. An addict. I wanted you to have better options than me. I thought I was saving you."

I couldn't help it. I scoffed, the sound halfway between a laugh and a snort. "It didn't do a bit of good, Mom. If you wanted to save

25

me, you should have stayed with me. Then maybe, just maybe, things could have been better for both of us but you didn't save me." I stopped, shored myself up. *Save me. I was right, she was spouting a load of crap.* "You didn't save me at all. Not even a little bit."

I turned and walked away, not letting her say anymore, quickly leaving her behind. I found my shopping cart and checked out, heading back to the bakery, hoping she would stay away.

Chapter Seven

By Sunday morning, the bakery and the apartment were as clean as they were going to get. Three days of cleaning had left me exhausted. On top of all the cleaning, Mallie had sent me out with her interior designer -- Luz's sister Isabel. The money my grandfather had left me wasn't going to stretch far but I quickly realized that Isabel was a master of second-hand shopping. We hit garage sales, estate sales, and consignment shops. Everything we'd found had been in rough shape but she'd gotten prices knocked down and made deal after deal. I already had furniture in the master bedroom. Nothing fancy but it was more than good enough for me.

Every day while I'd worked I'd ignored three things: the rapidly approaching Sunday, the boxes of family memories filling the utility room, and the frequent appearances of my mother in the square across the street. Mom had been the hardest thing to ignore. At random moments over the past three days I'd look out the front windows and she'd be there. Reading a book. Eating breakfast or lunch. Sometimes even eating an ice cream cone. I had to admire her persistence, but I still wasn't ready to deal with her. The boxes too, were always there, waiting to be dealt with. After years of zero family in my life I suddenly felt surrounded by it.

I scanned the square for my mom as I nursed a glass of milk and watched the city start to creep awake and get moving. *She's not there for once. Good.* I went back to watching the city come alive. Cars were just starting to venture out, each one heading to their normal Sunday morning spots. Church or breakfast out or one of another countless destinations. I carried my empty glass to the master bathroom, rinsing it and setting it aside. I'd return it to the bakery kitchen on my way to church.

Church. I didn't want to go. I didn't want to go anywhere today. It had been a good few days, but I was worn down and really wanted to spend the morning in my new bed with my new cat reading a book and napping. A deal was a deal though. If I was going to complete my year here, I had to stick to Harry's terms. So here I was, getting ready for church.

As I showered, brushed my teeth, and walked through all the other steps required for attending Sunday services I tried to remember the last time I'd gone to a church for a worship service. I'd been to meetings and weddings held in churches over the years but for just a regular Sunday service... I couldn't remember the last time. It had to have been when I was still a teen. I know I hadn't gone on my own.

I dug through a box of my clothes for something to wear and thought back, trying to remember any church visits. Mom had never taken me so a lot of years were ruled out right away. I'd gone into foster care at twelve. I know at least one foster family had been church goers. One visit came back to me with a jolt, crisp and clear. My foster mom had taken me to a local thrift store to shop for clothes. I could remember her grumbling about how I'd been sent to them with two changes of clothes and nothing more. She'd drug me to the thrift store and shoved outfit after outfit on me. I'd worn one of the new-to-me dresses on my first Sunday with them. She'd dropped me off at Sunday school before going to work in the nursery. I had walked into the classroom feeling like I belonged for the first time ever. My dress looked like the ones the other girls wore. I had just known I was going to fit in, make new friends, maybe get a chance at something like the happy normal lives I'd grown up watching on TV. At least I'd thought those things until one of the girls pointed at my dress and called out to one of her friends. *Didn't that used to be your dress, Sarah?* Her friend had immediately confirmed it -- I was wearing her old dress. The whole group of girls had all dissolved into laughter. I'd raced out of the classroom and had hidden in a closet until it was time for big church. I'd kept doing the same thing Sunday after Sunday until my foster family moved out of state the next year and I'd gone back into the system.

I paused as I started to leave the bedroom, catching a glimpse of myself in the mirrored closet doors. For a moment I saw the fearful girl I'd been. On the wrong side of chubby with carrot orange hair and a thrift store dress. I had been an outsider from the moment I'd stepped through the door back then. They had known... somehow they had all known from the very beginning. I wasn't like them. It was like they could tell I'd grown up sleeping in motel rooms, cars, and homeless shelters instead of in a proper bed in a proper home.

I stared at the woman in the mirror before me and reminded myself of how far I'd come. I hadn't tried to fit in anywhere for years and I wasn't going to start today. My hair, still bright red orange was a messy nest of waves, tangled together into a haphazard bun. I looked past my hair to my outfit, wondering what the church ladies would think. As I'd grown up I'd stuck to thrift store clothes, but I'd learned to look for vintage rather than just cheap and used. The form fitting vintage maxi dress I'd dug out of a box was a riot of fall colors -- all greens and golds in a fun geometric print. It was straight out of the seventies and I loved it. I expected to be the most brightly colored person in the Rio Verde Baptist Church.

"I look like a box of Crayons," I said to my reflection. Behind me, a squeaky meow sounded in agreement. The cat. When he'd curled up on the sleeping bag my first night here I'd realized he wasn't going anywhere. So I'd named him and bought him food and supplies and made him part of my family. When Isabel, Mallie, and I had put up the white wrought iron bed frame then crowned it with the best mattress I'd ever slept on, BC the Bakery Cat had gotten comfortable the moment we'd left the room. Now he slept there most of the day and purred me to sleep every night. I was officially a cat lady. I scratched his ears then grabbed my purse, heading out, every step slow and reluctant.

By the time I'd navigated the route to the church and found a parking spot, my I-don't-care-about-fitting-in-confidence had melted away. The moment the big red brick church appeared in front of me I was a nervous kid all over again, certain everyone would stare and point and whisper when I walked in. I jumped when my cell phone chimed.

"What's the hold up?"

It was Will. My warden. Making certain I stuck to the terms of the will. Run the bakery for one year. Go to church each Sunday. Stay put. Be an Abbott -- whatever that meant. I didn't want to like him but I did. There was just something about him. I couldn't not like him.

I stared at the church. The front doors, massive carved wood slabs, were wide open, a steady stream of people passing through them. I decided to be honest. "I don't want to go in there."

"So I gathered. Why?" Will appeared in the parking lot in front of the Bronco. I slipped out and walked over to him, each of us hanging up our cell phones. He studied me, those soft brown eyes intense behind the windows of his glasses. "They're just a bunch of Baptists. Mostly harmless. My dad's the preacher. He makes sure everyone plays nice. You don't have to be a devout person to come worship with us. Or do you not..."

He didn't finish the question but I heard it clearly in my head. *Do you not believe in God?* I didn't know how to answer him. No one could have lived my life and not have some sort of belief in a higher power. My belief was an abstract thing. Just like I believed that each snowflake was different. I knew it was true but I didn't confirm it. I couldn't say any of it to him. I didn't trust him enough yet even though something inside of me told me that I could trust him. I wasn't there yet. So instead I just shook my head no and looked away from him.

"Okay then. Let's go inside. We'll miss the service. I hate being late."

He reached out and caught my trailing hand, trying to tug me forward but I resisted. "I can't, Will. Just give me a pass. Just one. Just today. I'll get it together and come next week, I promise."

"That would violate the terms of Harry's will." His voice was stern and scolding but there was kindness on his face.

To my embarrassment my eyes filled with tears and my throat tightened. Panic rose inside me, the scared kid inside me taking over. I wanted to find another closet to hide in and avoid this whole thing.

"Please, Will." My voice was just a whisper, almost lost in the windy morning. I pushed at my eyes with my free hand, catching the tears before they could betray me and slip down my cheeks. Will caught the gesture and dropped my hand, his face softening. He looked over his shoulder as the last of the people walked through the big doors.

"They can get by without me today," he said as he tugged off his tie. "Let's go for a drive." He walked back to his car, tucked just to the right of my own. I could only stand there and watch. The change in him, the shift from all business to relaxed church-skipper had been impressively abrupt. I wondered about him. Who was this guy? Banker? Churchgoer? Something told me there was a lot more to Will Bell than it appeared. He was a man of many layers.

"Are you coming or not?" He stood beside the car, passenger door open, waiting for me. He'd tossed his tie inside and shed his jacket while I'd stayed frozen in place. He smiled at me, and the warm, kind smile decided things for me. I'd much rather figure him out than go inside the intimidating building.

"Yeah, I'm coming." I returned his smile, relief flooding me as I climbed into his car.

Chapter Eight

We left the church behind, driving away down the mostly empty street. An awkward silence settled over us. I'd talked to Will about money stuff plenty. I'd even shared a few personal details. I'd never been alone with him in such close quarters. It made me feel fidgety inside.

"So. Where are we going? Are you planning to drive me into the middle of nowhere and murder me?" My off the wall question made me flush. I wasn't sure why I'd blurted it out. It got a soft chuckle out of Will though so I didn't feel too embarrassed.

"No. Well, maybe no." He winked at me when I glanced over at him.

"You're not being very comforting. Seriously, where are we going?"

"Just to drive around a bit. I don't think you've seen much of the town yet. It seems like you've spent every waking moment working on the bakery."

"Stalker." He laughed again.

"I do two doors down."

"Ah. Good point." I looked over at him for a moment, just watching him as he turned away from the church and headed back toward the center of town. "You love this town, don't you?"

"I do. Mom and Dad moved us here when I was ten and my big brother Jackson was thirteen. It was a big change. We'd been in the Atlanta area my whole life. Here, though, Dad could lead his own church. That wasn't going to ever happen back in Georgia."

"Why?" I couldn't imagine why little Rio Verde would offer more opportunities than big Atlanta.

He was quiet for a moment and then dodged the question, pointing out some of the newer businesses in town. A yoga studio and an art gallery with several daring paintings displayed in the front window. Displaying paintings with nudity and graphic violence in such a way was gutsy in any town. The art was beautiful -- meant to shock and challenge the viewer, but beautiful. I wondered if the church ladies had protested the display or declared it to be the work of the devil like they did in 1980's movies. I expected Will to look away or distract me from the gallery but he didn't.

"Those are by several local artists," he said as we stopped at the red light right in front of the gallery. "The woman who painted the nudes was my high school English teacher. Not what you'd expect from a woman who looked like a 1950's housewife."

I laughed at his story as we drove away. He was right. I couldn't picture a woman who, in my mind, looked like Donna Reed painting the bold paintings.

As we worked our way through the town we bounced from commercial area to commercial area. Will pointed out brew pubs, a tattoo shop, and even a wine tasting room. There was also an organic grocery store and a vegan restaurant. It wasn't like I'd thought it would be. I'd pictured a quaint but kind of backward small town. Will was showing me it wasn't backward at all. It was unique and special.

"Are you ever going to tell me why?" I asked as we left the city, heading toward the slow, tree-lined river wandering through the countryside to the south.

"He's a black man married to a white woman. When I was a kid, I thought it was just a race thing keeping him from advancing to a bigger role at our church. Last year though Mom came clean. Her father, mine and Mallie's grandfather, had been in the Klan. He was a Grand Giant, whatever that is. I don't really want to know. She and Dad had always kept it quiet but I guess folks always found out. Which explained why they jumped at the chance to take over the church here. It's a little town but it's one of the most colorblind places I've ever seen. They don't see Dad's skin. They just see a man of God."

I didn't say anything. I just sat there and processed what he'd said. It made me wish I'd grown up here. Maybe I would have been

33

something more than a foster kid with a junkie mom. I couldn't help but feel a little jealous. My focus shifted as Will pulled into a parking spot beside a big riverside park. Tucked along the river which gave the city its name, the park was full of shade trees, picnic tables, and playground equipment. It was deserted on this quiet morning. Will turned off the car and stepped out, giving me no choice but to follow him as he headed down a gravel path.

I glanced back at the car, then at the gravel path and down at my high heeled sandals. I kicked them off and set them on the hood of Will's car and went after him. The gravel had just started to warm in the morning sun. I paused, digging my toes into the tiny pebbles. There was something soothing about the smooth stones surrounding my feet. I closed my eyes, tipping my face toward the sun. It was a beautiful morning. As I stood there the anxiety my attempted church visit had created started to melt out of me. A deep breath pushed it away for good and I opened my eyes and headed after Will.

"Thank you," I said when I reached the end of the trail. Will looked up from the bench he'd claimed, smiled, and turned back to watching the river flow past. "I haven't had an anxiety attack in a long time. Thanks for getting me out of there before I lost it."

I sat next to him and turned to watch him instead of the lazy river.

"I used to work with the youth at the church. I had a kid who was prone to those sorts of things. I recognized the signs."

"Well thank you. Just when you think you've got a handle on things..." I didn't finish, instead looking away for a moment at the muddy water drifting by below us.

"You inherit a bakery and your life goes off in a new, scary direction."

"Pretty much." I relaxed back into the bench, taking in the peaceful place Will had brought me to. The bench he'd picked was up on a high bank above the river. Tall, shady trees surrounded us. Across the bank were more trees then wide open prairie. I'd lived all over the place but this was my first chance to call Texas home. It was different here. A different kind of nature. A different kind of people. A different pace of life. How I ended up here was kind of strange but I couldn't help but think that a year here could be nice.

"Why'd you take this on, Will? Helping my grandfather. Helping me."

"I prayed about taking on this role when Harry asked me to. It was a big job and something I'd never done before. Tracking you down. Learning about running a bakery so I could advise you when I did find you. Everything was more than a little overwhelming." He shifted, turning on the bench to face me. "When he got sick, I was only working part time at the bank and part time at the church, working with the kids. I'd been helping him with his books on the side for years. Then the church found a husband and wife team to lead the youth full time. So I went on full time at the bank and started stopping by the bakery every day for lunch or a loaf of bread. I got to be good friends with him. It freaked me out when he asked me to handle his estate though."

A splash in the river caught our attention, both of us looking out at the water. A fish jumped, then another, then everything went quiet again.

"So I prayed about it and prayed about it. Talked to my dad about it. My Uncle Jonah too. Even my brother. Everyone said the same things. This was a chance for me to help someone and that was the push I needed. I'm good at numbers. Dad always told us it was our job to use our gifts to work for God. This was my chance."

Will went silent again, looking down at the bench. He'd been turning a stick over and over in his hands while he spoke. When it broke his fingers idly searched around for something to fiddle with. He turned his head, watching the river again, while I watched his hands. They eventually found the folds of my dress, his long, thin fingers twisting the fabric. I cleared my throat, drawing his focus back to me. When he turned back to me I glanced down. He followed my gaze and flushed when he realized he what he was playing with.

"Sorry. It's a very pretty dress."

"Thanks."

The peaceful moment was shattered by the ring of his cell phone. He rose, tugging it out of his shirt pocket and walked away. I rose too, walking back to the car while he talked to the caller. It had been a good morning, but it was time to get back on with the day. I was sure Will had places to go. So did I. I needed to go get ready to open the bakery up on Tuesday. In a few moments Will was coming up the path toward me, car keys in hand.

"Time to go back?"

"Yup. Sundays are for family lunch. I've got to go. You should come too. You can help explain why I wasn't in church. Maybe keep me out of trouble."

"Oh no. Just drop me back at my truck. I need to go back to work. I'm not ready to open for business yet. I've never been good at parents or getting people out of trouble."

"Deal. Next Sunday, I'll meet you at the church. You can sit with me and Mallie and our families. It won't be scary. I promise."

"Deal." I thought about next Sunday and didn't feel the panic rise up inside. I was still unsure about the whole going to church thing but I felt like it wouldn't be so scary with Will by my side.

Chapter Nine

I worked in my grandfather's office most of the afternoon, going through his old recipe books, trying to decide what to put on the menu. He'd stuck to simple breads and cookies but those had never been my thing. I'd always gone for unique flavors in my desserts. Rosemary cookies. Apricot ginger scones. I loved making breakfast breads and bars too. Cinnamon bread, sausage and cheese stuffed rolls. I weighed his recipes against my own, trying to find a balance between things Rio Verde was used to seeing and things I loved making. Then I tried to figure out how I was going to make all of it by myself while still running the register and dealing with customers.

In the back of my head all day my conversation with Will had run on repeat. I finally took a break from my lists and recipes to think about everything. His comments about using your gifts for God stuck out the most. No one had ever talked about God in such a way to me before. Mallie too had talked about God in a way brand new to me. To me it was as though both of them saw God as a friend. More than a friend. An anchor. A certainty. I pulled myself back up to the desk, trying to refocus. Certainties were pretty foreign to me. They'd especially been scarce lately. My world had gone upside down lately. Totally upside down. Lost my job. Lost my apartment. Got a letter that changed everything. Saw my mom again. I looked at the mess on the desk and sighed. The only certainty I knew of now was that I needed to work ahead as much as possible.

BC meowed at me from his spot on the bookcase across from the desk. He'd claimed an empty shelf as his the moment I'd sat down at the desk.

"Buddy, you're going to need to learn how to bake if you're sticking around. I'm going to need a hand around here." He meowed again and closed his eyes. I wasn't going to get any useful work out of him today or probably ever. I flipped off the light, leaving him in darkness. Standing in the kitchen I debated about starting some bread or cookies tonight. When a yawn took over, leaving me swamped with tiredness I turned the kitchen light off too. I made the downstairs loop, checking all the doors, locking up, yawning the whole way. By the time I climbed the stairs to the apartment I was dragging. BC was waiting for me when I reached the bedroom.

As I lay in bed watching the stars wink on outside my window, more of my morning with Will came back to me. The way he'd talked about my grandfather had stuck with me too. It was such a departure from the man Mom had told me about when I was a kid. She'd made him out to be some sort of monster who had chased his daughter and granddaughter away from the only home they'd had. The man Will had talked about didn't seem capable of such a thing. A man who would leave his bakery to the granddaughter he'd never known... he couldn't have been like Mom had described.

My last thought before falling asleep was of the boxes crowding the laundry room. I'd made a path through them to the washer and dryer and the back door. I hadn't opened a one though. I wondered, as sleep claimed me, what was hiding in those boxes. If I dove into them, would I be able to understand the family I'd never known?

*****

"Can you make a wedding cake?"

The question pulled my focus from the cookie dough before me. I looked up as Mallie walked into the kitchen. Behind her I could see her crew heading upstairs to demo what was left of my kitchen. I refocused on her with a smile.

"I sure can. Making cakes is my thing. Do you need one?"

I couldn't help but smile as Mallie charged into the kitchen, leaving a trail of dust and dirt behind her. I'd worked in close to two dozen bakeries since I was a teen. I'd spoken to a lot of brides. This was my first bride with a tool belt around her waist. She climbed onto

38

one of the stools at the marble topped island in the center of the bakery and cast a lustful glance at the basket of cookies sitting in the center.

"Go ahead, have some. Try to keep your dust and dirt to yourself though. I'm baking here." She looked behind her, flushing when she saw the dirt she'd tracked in.

"I'll clean that up, I promise."

"No you won't. You'll go back up to work. I'll clean it up." I smiled at her, softening my words with the gesture. I wasn't mad. I wanted her to know.

"Okay, boss," she said with a laugh. "Before I go, can we talk about a cake?" I nodded and resumed scooping out cookie dough. I was almost finished and didn't want to stop. Mallie snatched a cookie from the basket, giving it a sniff then taking a huge bite. I turned away, picking up the full cookie sheet, picked up another one, and took them to the fridge where they could wait a while.

"Oh my gosh," Mallie said around a mouthful of cookie. "What are these?"

"What do you think they are?"

"They look like pumpkin but there's something else."

"Hazelnut."

"Yes. With chocolate chips too."

"You nailed it. My own creation. It's a little soon for fall flavors but I was craving them." I walked past her into the office, returning with a pad and pencil. I grabbed a cookie for myself as I took a seat across the island from her. Taking a bite, I savored the combination of flavors. The medley was my favorite. It brought to mind crisp air, falling leaves, and shorter days. Fall had always been my favorite season and even though it was just the end of August, I was already getting eager for sweaters, scarves, and all things fall. I finished the cookie and dusted the crumbs off my fingertips, smiling when Mallie snatched a second cookie from the basket.

"I can't stop," she said, breaking the cookie in half then popping a piece into her mouth.

"I have the same problem." I took a second one myself, laughing when Mallie and I locked eyes then looked at the cookies again. I reached behind me and grabbed a towel off the counter, covering the cookies, removing temptation to a certain degree. "Okay. Let's talk cake. First things first. How many people are coming?"

"We're looking at between two fifty and three hundred."

"Dang, Mallie, you invite the whole town?"

She sighed and rolled her eyes. "Just about. Dad's the oldest of four kids. All his younger siblings have several kids. Plus, Tres has a big family too. Then when you take into account both our families are local business owners and so are Tres and I. The list got out of control super fast."

"No one from your Mom's side of the family?"

"Just Aunt Jo, Uncle Noah, Jackson, his wife and kids, and Will. Both of my mom's folks were gone before I was five. I never knew them. It's no great loss though. From what I've been told they weren't very nice people."

"I'm sorry. Will mentioned them to me." I wasn't sure what to say. I thought about my own messed up family. Sure, the state of Nevada had raised me and I didn't know who my dad was and I'd never met ninety-nine percent of my family. Yet here was Mallie, planning her wedding without her mom, without a whole branch of her family tree. All of my baggage was pretty small when I put it into perspective.

"Really? Will told you? He doesn't talk about it much. Even to me and we're pretty tight." She smiled a little half smile. It told me she was thinking about what Will confiding in me meant. She refocused quickly, adding, "It's okay. You can't miss people you never knew, right?"

"I don't know." I looked down at my pad, thinking about all the family I'd never known. "I have kinda always missed my dad. Or who I imagined he would be. I miss my grandparents, too, or I miss what it would have been like to know them. It's silly. I'm a grown ass woman but I still wish I'd had something more like a normal family."

Mallie looked at me, her sky blue eyes serious. "Sounds like we need to have a girls night. Swap stories."

"You are on. First though, let's talk about your wedding cake. It's going to be a big one."

"Huge?"

"I'll have to hire extra help to carry the darn thing."

"Awesome. We'll feed all of Rio Verde with it."

We burst out laughing and I whipped the towel off the basket of cookies. "We're going to need more sugar if we're going to hash out this cake." We both reached for a cookie and got down to business.

Chapter Ten

I heard the bell over the front door tinkle softly as my last customer of the day left. She held up a half-eaten cookie and called thank you as she disappeared into the evening. I slid off the stool behind the register, trudging to the front door, flipping the sign over to CLOSED and lowering the blinds in the windows. I needed to clean up. Close out the register. Put up everything I hadn't sold. Instead I boosted myself up onto the long counter and laid down. Opening day had done me in. Just as I closed my eyes I heard the front door open, the sleigh bells I'd hung on it jingling happily.

"I'm closed," I muttered, not opening my eyes.

"How'd your first day go?"

It was Will. I'd get up for him. For a little bit at least.

"Well. Very well. I think most people wanted to get a look at the long lost Abbott heir. They bought things while they were here though so let them come look." I slid off the counter and reached inside the display case. "Want some cookies?"

Will didn't need to be asked twice. Like his cousin he had a sweet tooth. He took two of the oatmeal chocolate chip cookies I'd offered.

"Nice ink," he said over a mouthful of cookie.

I glanced down, for a moment not sure what he was talking about. Then I caught the edge of my one and only tattoo in the corner of my eye. I'd forgotten how visible it was when I was in my normal baking uniform of kaki cargo pants and a tank top. I'd started out the day in a chef's coat, looking all professional. I'd burned it on a hot cookie sheet and tossed it aside around noon. I turned so he could see more of it and smiled.

"Thanks. I'm fond of it."

He leaned closer, studying it. From my back the branches of a tree stretched out, crossing over my left shoulder and down my bicep. It was covered in faint pink flowers and a scattering of tiny green leaves.

"Dogwood, right?"

"Yeah. Most people think it's a cherry tree. It's from a real tree my friend Carson and I found when we were on a backpacking trip. I have a photo of me sitting under it in the office. It's too... PG13 to display, but I love it so I put it where I can look at it."

He followed me to the office, his eyes going wide when I handed him the small framed photo. It was a single blooming dogwood along the edge of a forest. The day had been cloudy so the light was soft, making it look like it was about to rain. Carson, always the photographer, had demanded I be his model for the photo. We'd hiked ten miles before we'd found the tree and I was sweaty, dirty, and beat but I'd obliged him, stripping down to just my undies and sitting below the tree. My bare back was to the camera and you couldn't see a thing. There was something about the photo that made most people feel like they were seeing something they shouldn't. I loved it though. I'd felt beautiful in that moment and every time I looked at it I felt beautiful again.

"Wow."

"You see why I can't put it where anyone can just stumble across it."

"Yeah. It's... amazing but very intimate. Like the photographer caught a moment no one was meant to see."

"Just what Carson was going for, but it's posed. I was also sweaty and dirty. We'd been hiking all day."

"Who's Carson?" I caught the edge of jealousy in his voice as I set the photo down and gave him a look as I walked past him back into the kitchen.

"Just an old friend. We hiked the Appalachian Trail together a few years ago. He wanted to just unplug from society and refocus himself. I wanted to quit drinking. So he invited me to come along.

Seven months of hiking without any handy bars or liquor stores. It was a great way to get sober. I got the tattoo to celebrate getting my life on track." As I spoke I started cleaning the kitchen. I wasn't sure why the story had poured out of me but I'd just felt like Will had needed to know the back story and who Carson was. "I haven't seen Carson since then. I moved out to Portland on a whim not long after we finished the trail. He's one of those friends who drifts in and out of your life. He'll drift back in one of these days. You know what I mean? Surely you've had a friend or two like that."

"He was never a boyfriend?"

Will caught me off guard with the question. I laughed, I couldn't help it. The idea was crazy to me. "No. Carson is the closest thing I've ever had to a brother. We're way too similar to ever be anything more than friends."

Before I could ask him why he wanted to know the twinkle of the front door echoed through the empty bakery.

"I'm sorry, but I just closed for the day," I called out, heading into the storefront. I froze when I walked through the doorway and saw who was standing there. "Son. Of. A. Biscuit." I must have spoken louder than I'd intended to because not only did I hear Will start toward me, but the woman before me winced, my words hitting her with more intensity than I'd wanted.

"Joy." She took two hesitant steps toward me. "Please."

"No. No, Mom. Not now. It's been a long damn day. I can't handle you right now." I could keep the anger out of my voice -- it was gone. Since the day at Walmart I'd let go of every ounce of my anger. I still loved her, I had realized. However, I was so disappointed in her and so distrustful. I just knew if I let her back into my life she'd end up disappearing again. The idea of going through all of that again just wore me out.

"We need to talk about this." She held up the envelope from the lawyer's office. The twin to the one I'd gotten. I had to admit, I wanted to know what her envelope said.

"Fine. Just leave it here. I'll read it. Then we'll talk. Much later."

She moved, closing the distance between us. I hadn't been this close to her since she'd abandoned me at a bus station in Las Vegas. Even in Walmart she hadn't come this close. I could have reached out to hug her if I'd wanted to -- or to slap her. I didn't want to do either, didn't want to touch her at all. She took advantage of the closeness -- reaching out, touching my cheek. I jerked away -- the gesture too familiar. Too welcome. Too much like a trap.

"You've grown into a beautiful woman, Joy. I'm sorry I wasn't there."

"Yeah, well me too but you made your choice." My voice was low as I tried to keep Will from hearing everything. I took the envelope from her and stepped back again, retreating a bit. I looked at her as she stood there, guilt hanging on her like a heavy coat. I tried to feel sorry for her but I was just too worn out with her.

"Joy? Are you okay?" It was Will. I felt him come to stand behind me, laying a hand on the small of my back. The sad little girl inside me was a bit stronger at his touch. I realized for once I wasn't standing on my own. I had a circle of new friends who I was pretty sure had my back.

"I'm good," I said. I meant it too. She couldn't hurt me again. She could vanish again and I'd be okay. I'd survived it once and I could a second time.

"Will, meet Susan Abbott." He stared at me, his unspoken question all over his face -- *Is she your mom?*

I nodded, answering him. I smiled for a half second as he remembered his manners. "Ma'am," he said, nodding to her.

"Is this your husband, honey?"

I glanced over at Will, surprised to see him glance at me. The flutter in my stomach when our eyes met didn't surprise me this time. It had started happening every time I met his eyes. I pushed it aside though. "No, this is Will. Will Bell. He's my..."

"Friend and business manager." Will defined his role for me and stepped around me, reaching out to shake her hand.

She smiled and took his hand. "Oh I met your mother when I got to town the other day. She's such a sweet woman."

"That's not something most people call my mom. Usually they aren't so kind."

She laughed, the noise filled the empty bakery and punched me right in the heart. Her laugh was still the same. Those old feelings of missing my mom flooded me, fighting with the disappointment I'd been holding between us. I pushed it away and made myself focus on the present.

"What else do you need, Mom?" My words broke the mood, taking away the brief moment of lightness. I watched as she gathered herself.

"I'll just go then. I've obviously interrupted your evening. My cell number is on the envelope. Call me when you're ready to talk."

I started to speak but my words froze in my throat. I could only stand there and watch her go back through the door, walk across the empty street, and get into a small car. When the taillights had vanished around a corner I moved again, sucking in a huge lungful of air and stepping toward the front door.

"Wow."

Will looked over at me, concerned in his coffee colored eyes. "Wow?"

"That was my mom."

"Yes it was."

"Wow."

"How long has it been?"

"Six days. Before then though, twenty years. She left me at a bus station when I was just twelve, saying she'd be right back. I never saw her again."

"Oh, okay. I get the wow now. Damn."

"Exactly."

Chapter Eleven

It took almost an hour to convince Will I wasn't going to have a breakdown just because my mom had walked back into my life. I had to promise I wasn't going to read her letter and lay awake all night. Once he was sure I was only going to eat dinner and go to bed early he headed home, leaving BC and I alone in the bakery. I finished cleaning up, ran the day's deposit over to the bank, grabbed an apple for my dinner, and then finally climbed the stairs up to the apartment.

Mallie's crew had made a big dent in the kitchen project while I'd been working in the bakery. All of the ruined cabinetry was gone, the black soot on the brick wall the only thing left. BC immediately inspected everything they'd left behind, climbing one of the ladders then tunneling through the drop cloths spread across most of the floor. I stood there, watching him poke around, trying to process the day. When I leaned back on the utility room door it creaked open and I stumbled backward into the room. Boxes and boxes. All labeled in what I knew was Will's handwriting.

Right beside the door was a stack of boxes all labeled "Books." I pulled the top box open, taking the first book my hand landed on. I struggled to lift out what turned out to be a massive leather-bound book. I bit into my apple, freeing up my other hand and gently cradled the nearly four inch wide book. Stepping into a beam of late day sunlight, I tipped the cover to the light. *Holy Bible.*

"Wow," I muttered around the apple. Mallie's words came to me. *A God thing.* I knew I'd pulled the utility room door closed before I'd gone to work in the morning. No one working on the remodel would have had a reason to go in there. They'd been going up and down the interior stairs all day. Maybe it had been a God thing. Maybe the door opened so I'd find the Bible. I held it to my chest and took the apple from my mouth. As I chewed, I tugged the door shut properly and headed to the bedroom, depositing the Bible on the bed. In a few short moments I was showered and ready for bed. I picked up the Bible and settled back against my mountain of pillows.

It was a beautiful old book. I laid it across my crossed legs, carefully cleaning a bit of dust off the cover. Tarnished brass guards protected the corners of the front and back covers. The spine and front cover were embossed with beautiful details. I ran a finger over some of the decoration, more dust coming away revealing a hint of gold on the mahogany leather. It was latched shut with two brass clasps, both tarnished like the decorative corners. I could imagine it new. All the brass shiny and golden. The cover soft, new leather, the gold details on it sharp and clear. I wondered how old it was and where it had come from. Carefully I opened one latch and then the other, holding my breath as I opened the cover. The title page answered both my questions. *1890* and the name of a London press gave me an age and an origin. I turned a few pages and found a list of family records. Marriages, births, and then deaths all recorded in a wide range of handwritings. At the end of the list of births I was shocked to find my own name.

A crash from the kitchen pulled my focus off the Bible. Seconds later BC shot into the bedroom, vaulting onto the bed, a blur of black and white.

"What did you do?"

He responded with a meow and flopped onto his side, sighing and starting to purr.

"Weirdo," I said as I reached over and ran my fingers through his long fur. He purred louder and flipped onto his back. I knew better than to venture onto his belly. He'd love the affection for maybe five seconds then he would bite the crap out of me. So instead I removed my hand and leaned back, returning to my exploration of what was obviously my family Bible.

I turned the pages at random, feeling along the edges until I found a gap or a folded corner. Each time I found something sandwiched between the pages. A ribbon of lace and a single dried purple flower. Old advertisements. Two locks of hair braided into circles and glued to a slip of heavy paper, a trio of letters below each one. A bus ticket for someone named Walter Abbott dated 1912. More and more dried flowers. Newspaper clippings and obituaries. Programs from church services. Memories. It was filled with memories from generations of Abbotts. It made me light headed to think of all the history I could learn from the items tucked into the Bible. I closed it gently, tracing the edges of the gilt pages a final time as I yawned so hard my eyes watered. My fingertips grazed over something small and soft just barely poking out of the top of the Bible. I leaned over, searching for what I'd felt and saw a tiny sliver of deep blue. With my fingernail I separated the pages around it, opening the Bible to find a slim blue velvet ribbon someone had used as a bookmark. I scanned the pages and found a single underlined verse.

"Exodus 14:14," I read aloud. "Jehovah will fight for you, and ye shall be still." I wondered about the meaning of the simple verse and reached for my phone on the nightstand. A quick internet search led me to a more modern translation.

"The Lord will fight for you; you need only to be still." I put away my phone and closed the Bible, setting it on the bottom shelf of the nightstand. As I lay back, letting my tiredness pull me toward sleep I thought about those last two words. Being still had never been my strong suit. I'd always been ready to move, getting restless after too long at a job or in a town. Thanks to my grandfather's will I was getting a forced lesson on being still. I was starting to believe in Mallie's "God thing." It had taken a lot of seemingly random moments to get me here -- to get me to open the Bible and read that one verse. Maybe, just maybe, it was time to be still.

Chapter Twelve

"I can do this." I whispered the words to myself as I stared at the church before me. The week had flown by. It had been a blur of cookies, cakes, and bread. Each day filled with customers, the constant ring of the front door's bells, and bangs and crashes from the second floor. Sunday had arrived before I was ready for it. My heart thudded in my chest so I took a deep breath, trying to settle it down. From either side of the Bronco people flowed past. Everyone was intent on their destination, the big church dominating my view. The hulking structure of red brick sat in the center of the ocean of asphalt, cars all around it. As churches went it was pretty normal looking. Big wooden doors at the front entrance, big white columns across the front. Along the sides and out of my view were tall stained glassed windows depicting the traditional Biblical scenes -- Mary and baby Jesus, angels doing angel stuff, and so on. I knew there also had to be Sunday School classrooms, offices, meeting rooms, and more. It was a just normal church I told myself over and over. Every inch of me still dreaded going inside. I hoped Will would appear and give me another reprieve but I didn't think it would be likely.

"I can do this," I whispered again, finally slipping out of the truck and walking through the emptying parking lot. I paused when I passed a minivan, checking my appearance in the reflection. I'd done the best I could. I'd tamed my unruly rust-colored waves into a thick braid. I'd traded my tank top, cargo pants, and tennis shoes for the one of the few nice dresses I owned, something tamer than the print dress I'd tried to wear on my first attempt to come to church. The vintage denim dress was one of my favorites. Simple, knee length, and best of all comfortable. I'd found some sandals and lightweight cardigan the color of heavy cream in one of my boxes. I hoped I looked okay. I didn't know what was okay in church fashion. In my head I felt like I should be wearing an ankle length skirt with a sweater set or something else super conservative.

I reminded myself once more that I could do this. I'd cleaned the bakery top to bottom on my own. I was running it all on my own, baking night and day. I'd handled a lot of big stuff in the past couple of weeks. I could do this. I could handle church. Then I reminded myself that I had to or I'd lose the bakery. The thought made my heart clench. It was all so overwhelming. I'd been drifting around for my whole life. Staying still felt like giving up. It felt like drowning. Sighing, I squared my shoulders and closed the final distance to the big front doors determined to see this through. Even if it felt scary as hell.

As I passed through the open doors I took a paper program from two men in their Sunday best -- polished boots, slacks and matching straw cowboy hats. Each welcomed me and said they were happy to see me. I wanted to believe them but a snarky voice inside me said they were required to say those same things to everyone. I followed the crowd toward the sanctuary, stopping when I walked inside. It didn't look like a normal church inside. Or what I'd thought a normal church would look like. There were no hard wooden pews. Instead there was row after row of padded, comfortable looking chairs more like what you'd see in a waiting room at a doctor's office. On the stage there was no gown clad choir. Instead it looked more like the set up one would expect to see at a party. There was a set of drums, a keyboard, a big piano, and several guitars along with a handful of stand mounted microphones. This town just kept surprising me. It was never what I thought it was going to be. As the crowd moved around me I slipped into a seat at the back as fast as I could, ready to observe any other surprises the church might have.

"Nope. You're not going to hide."

I jumped when Will appeared behind me. I smiled up at Will, surprised to realize how happy I was to see him. In the sea of people, he was a familiar and friendly face. I was still a stranger in a strange land. He felt like a lifesaver.

Before I could speak Will stepped around the chairs and grabbed my hand, leaving me no choice but to follow him. My stomach sank when I realized he was leading me right to the front.

"No, Will, I'll be fine in the back. I like the back."

"You're sitting with your family."

I couldn't help but laugh, a short, snort of sarcasm I smothered before anyone beyond Will could hear it. "What family? My mom? My mystery father? I don't have a family."

My words stopped his purposeful steps. "Ouch. Yes you do. You just don't realize we're your family yet."

I stared at him in surprise. The idea hadn't occurred to me. My new friends. Did they really already count me as part of their family?

"I'm sorry. I didn't think..."

He smiled and shrugged off my apology. "No big deal. Come on. They're starting."

I looked around as he tugged me down the aisle. All around us people were getting settled in their chairs, visiting and laughing. Families, groups of friends and they all looked happy and relaxed and genuinely excited to be at church. Not a single one was looking at me and judging me. It was the first time I'd been in a church and not felt secret glances and whispered comments follow behind me. I felt a weight lift off me. I'd been so scared it would be just like I was a poor foster kid again. Judged before they'd known me.

Will stopped at the front of the church, steering me into a row. I realized we'd be sitting with someone who had to be his mother and froze. She looked so put together. Like a proper church lady. Sweater set and everything. There was no way she would look at me and not see through to the anxious, lost kid still hiding inside of me. To my surprise she stood and smiled and opened her arms and hugged me. The easy affection caught me off guard but the warmth of the gesture relaxed me in an instant. It was a mom-type hug -- comforting in a way that made me a bit sad when it ended. As the musicians took the stage and started to warm up, we sat. She leaned over and whispered how happy she was to meet me at last. Then she added that she was amazed at how much I looked like my mother. I felt my mouth open in shock, stunned to know that the preacher's wife would remember my mom, the bad girl who got knocked up at sixteen.

I thought about Mom as the music kicked into gear with a sudden guitar solo. Everyone around me stood up to sing along. I stood with them, not singing, but thinking instead. When she'd left me and I'd ended up in the system I'd taken every chance I'd had to try and find her. Any time I had gotten access to a computer I'd searched for her, scouring online newspaper articles for any mention of Susie Abbott. On the day I aged out of the system I went back to the bus station as if I could somehow follow her trail after six years. I'd never found her. I glanced around the church, wondering if she was here today. For the first time I wondered about her letter. What had my grandfather told her to do? What sort of sentence had he locked her into? And why was I thinking about her so much? I couldn't seem to stop myself. She slipped into my head at random moments every day.

The song ended and my focus shifted back to the present. A man close to my own age bounded to the stage, full of energy. He wore a tee shirt that said "Bibles and Biceps" with jeans and tennis shoes. Not what I expected to see in a church. I stifled a yawn as he welcomed everyone, gave some quick announcements and then encouraged the members to go greet any visitors they might see. I was thankful when a big group of visitors drew most everyone's attention, allowing me a chance to sit down and observe everyone. I continued to people watch during the rest of the music and then the sermon. I listened with half my brain, enjoying Will's father's engaging and powerful voice. His message was about foundations built on faith and the like. He discussed how we would all face storms in our life. Then he pointed out that, if a person had a firm foundation of faith, they'd be able to weather the storms with the help of the Lord. As he drew to a close he talked about putting down roots and standing still. He said building a foundation of faith without being still and letting God take the lead didn't work.

I heard it all -- every word. Even agreed with him. I saw his points clear as day. I knew I couldn't ever build anything if I kept running around the country. A part of me still stayed cynical though. He made it seem so simple but I knew reality was different. Staying put was hard and something I had learned to never trust. I was always waiting for the other shoe to drop. I was always waiting for the judging to start. I was always waiting for everything to fall apart again.

Chapter Thirteen

My plans to go back to the apartment and take a long nap after church were derailed by Will and his family. Mostly by Mallie. She'd demanded I come have lunch with them. Her dad Jonah had quickly agreed. Then Will had gotten on board, his mom and dad chiming in last. There was no putting them off. So instead of heading home I'd left my truck at the church and ridden shotgun in Will's car over to Mallie's house where I'd gotten a great meal from her dad and her aunt.

"I love your house, Mallie." I paused to admire the pretty front porch as I joined her on one of the matching porch swings. Her dad had given me a short Rio Verde history lesson over lunch, including the history of the house. His grandfather had built the stunning foursquare home when the town was still in its infancy. As we'd eaten I'd learned that the Andrews and the Abbotts had been some of Rio Verde's founding families. It hadn't been the afternoon I'd had planned but it wasn't so bad.

"It's kind of awesome, isn't it?" As she spoke she looked over her shoulder at the house, reaching out an arm to touch the deep gray siding. "I love pretty much every old house I see but this old gal will always be my favorite. I think growing up in a house so well cared for that it is practically a monument to architecture planted the seed for Andrews & Andrews Restoration."

"What about ballet? When your dad gave me a tour of the house I saw a photo of a ballet dancer that had to be you. Why did you give it up?" I looked over at her when I spoke, watching emotions flicker across her face. It was an odd mix of sadness, longing, and peace.

"Oh, God had other plans for me." She unfolded her long legs, stretching them out in front of the porch swing, making us rock a bit.

Reaching down she lifted the skirt of her dress, revealing scarred legs and a knee wrapped in a brace. "I had an accident, right after I graduated from Juilliard."

"I'm so sorry, Mallie." I looked away from her legs to the wide front yard. I'd stuck my foot in my mouth and didn't know what to do or how to make it better.

"Oh, don't be sorry. It took a while for me to realize it, but the accident was a good thing. It put me on a path back to Rio Verde. I would have never moved home after my mom passed if I had still been dancing. If I hadn't moved home I wouldn't get to work every day with my dad to save old houses. If I hadn't started working with my dad I wouldn't have got to work on Tres' house and we wouldn't be about to get married." She was quiet for a moment, touching her engagement ring as she thought. "It wasn't the path I would have chosen for my life. I'd rather my mom be here still. All in all, though, I'm happy to be where I am. I feel like things are right in my life for the first time since the accident. Truthfully, they're right for the first time since before the accident."

"Dang. I don't know what to say, Mallie. That's something else. I admire how well you've handled it all. I don't know if I would have had the same kind of grace through such a major trial."

"Oh, I didn't have much grace going through it all. I screwed up lots of things." She paused and looked down at the glass in her hand. For a second she was miles away.

"I was furious with God for a long time," she finally said. "I stayed distant from my family and friends for way too long. I hurt a lot of folks while I was wrapped up within my own tragedy. It took losing Mom..." Her voice broke and she paused again, gathering herself. "It took losing my mom to get me to let go of all the baggage I'd been carrying. It has been a rough year since then but my faith is stronger now than it ever was. Mom would be happy to know something so good came out of her death."

We slipped into an easy silence as Mallie reached out one of her long legs and touched the porch floor, pushing off and making the

56

swing start to sway. My own short legs could barely reach as we glided back and forth, the movement stirring the still air. Around us the neighborhood was quiet and peaceful. A distant dog started to bark and was joined by another then they fell silent. Behind us the muffled sound of the tv rumbled, white noise in the background of the day. I could hear voices coming from the house as everyone inside talked and laughed.

A breeze kicked up, the coolness making both Mallie and I shiver. Fall had arrived the day before with a cold front. Even though there was a chill in the air it was nice to sit outside and not sweat. The wind blasted us again, and I tucked my bare feet under me, trying to keep my toes warm. I smiled when Mallie did the same. We could have gone inside but instead we each sipped our glasses of ice tea and rocked back and forth, content on the porch.

"Speaking of mothers, how are things with your mom? I can't help but notice her stalking the bakery."

I lifted my tea, the ice cubes rattling against the almost empty glass as I sipped and bought myself some time. I wasn't sure how much to share with Mallie. I'd told Will a little bit about the screwed up relationship I had with my mom but it felt like Mallie was asking to know more than I'd ever shared with anyone. Having new friends who wanted to know about me and my life was new and foreign. First Will, now Mallie. I'd called her nosey the other day but I knew she wasn't just nosey. She really wanted to know about me. They both did.

"Things are... tense."

"Uh huh. I get it. How long has it been since you had a real conversation with her?"

Before I could answer her the front door squeaked open and Will joined us on the porch, pausing to give me a fresh glass of ice tea.

"Hey. Why does she get a new glass? Where is mine?"

Will dragged over a rocking chair joining us in the sunny corner of the porch.

"Your glass is in the kitchen. You can go get it anytime you want."

"But Will. My knee. The kitchen is so far."

He reached out a foot and pushed her hand away from her knee. "You're fine, brat."

She leaned over and gave him a soft punch in the shoulder. "Jerk."

I couldn't help but smile at the exchange. The two cousins, I had learned over lunch, were more like siblings. Around her, he shed his serious banker exterior and relaxed into what I had realized was more of the real Will. Teasing, laughing, and kind. Always kind.

"So, what were y'all talking about?" Will's question pulled me out of my head and back to the conversation I'd been hoping to avoid.

"Joy was just about to tell me what the deal is with her and her mom."

"Excellent. Did you read her letter yet, Joy?" Mallie's eye went wide at this new bit of information.

I squirmed as both of them stared at me, waiting for me to spin out a story. My heart thudded in my chest, so loud I was sure they could hear it. The old fear of being seen as the second coming of my troubled mother resurfaced as I fought down a growing panic. I reminded myself -- these people were trying to be my friends. I was a very different person from my mother. My inner voice whispered to me -- *Suck it up, girl. Be honest.*

"No I haven't. It's still sitting in the office where I left it Tuesday night." Mallie opened her mouth, sure to have a follow up question for my statement. For a split second I got scared that she'd give me a lecture about being responsible or something equally judgmental. I pushed those fears aside and instead answered any questions she might have before she could give them voice. "I'm just not ready to deal with her. I forgive her for what she did but it's been twenty years since I've had any sort of relationship with her. There's a lot of ground to make up. By both of us. I'm not even sure where to start." I knew the letter she'd left at the bakery was probably a good starting place but I couldn't bring myself to open it. I'd been ignoring it since she'd left it there.

"Twenty years? What happened?" It was Mallie who asked but I could see the question echoed on Will's face. Both had grown up with two loving parents. My childhood was a foreign thing to them.

"Up until recently, I hadn't seen her since I was twelve years old. She left me in a bus station in Las Vegas. She promised to come back but she never did. I spent the rest of my childhood as a ward of the state. I bounced around group homes and foster homes until I aged out of the system."

I left the truth hovering in the air before us. Mallie and Will just looked at me. Will had known that part of the story already though. I was happy he'd kept it to himself but I could tell he knew there was more to it I wasn't sharing. Mallie, however, was surprised, shock all over her face. It was a heavy fact, I knew, and hard for her to process. For me, it was a weight lifted. For the first time in a very long time I'd been honest about my past. Granted, there were a lot more truths there to be shared later. Just putting this one big truth out into the world left me feeling free and maybe one step closer to letting go of the regrets and shame I had drug around with me all these years.

Chapter Fourteen

"You look exhausted." It was Wednesday, only two days into my workweek. Will was right though, I was exhausted and I looked it. I'd caught my reflection in a glass bowl earlier. I was rocking some impressive dark circles under my eyes thanks to the fatigue in every inch of my body.

"Just what a girl wants to hear from a cute guy." I glanced over at Will when I spoke, daring to ignore the busy bakery for a second.

"You called me cute."

"I did not. You must be hearing things. Maybe you're not getting enough sleep."

He just stared a minute then took his glasses off, rubbing the bridge of his nose before putting the glasses back on. "How long do you think you'll be able to keep this up? You're going to have to do more than bake and sleep."

I knew he was right. The shop had been open less than two weeks and I was dying. My whole body hurt from the hours I was putting in. Most of the day I was on my feet, moving constantly. The bakery was busy every day from the moment I'd opened the door until I closed. Even though I baked during the day, running from the ovens to the register over and over, I still had to rise before dawn to get enough baked. Poor BC was getting almost no attention. I was running out of clean clothes. I hadn't been to the store since the Monday before I opened and both the cat and I were almost out of food.

Instead of answering him I yawned, so wide my jaw popped.

"Uh huh. Just what I thought." He walked away, disappearing into the office.

It was the first I'd seen him since Sunday. Three days since I'd seen someone I was growing very fond of. I told myself it was fine. Even though I was feeling more and more at home here, I was still planning on leaving in a year. The voice in my head was still telling me to run. So there was no point making long-term friendships. Or whatever Will and I were headed towards. Then today he'd come by today on his lunch break to check on things.

"How about I go over the books for you? Make sure things are going well financially." It was the third time he'd asked. I chanced a look over at him. The single butterfly leapt to attention in my stomach when he grabbed a cookie off a cooling rack and gave me a wink. I mentally ordered it to behave and looked away, my gaze landing on my mom. She'd been camped out on a bench in the square for around an hour, keeping an eye on the bakery while she read a book.

"If I hire help will you go back to work and leave me alone?"

"Maybe." He appeared beside me, carrying another cookie. Will followed my gaze and realized what I was thinking. "Your mom?"

"Sure. Why not? What could go wrong?"

"Hmm." He studied her, his soft brown eyes narrowed. I could almost see the wheels turning in his head.

"Hmm what?"

"Just trying to calculate the number of things that could go wrong."

"Shut up." I tried to shove him through the opening beside the cash register and into the front of the shop but was too tried to do more than make him take a step forward. "Go back to work."

Will strolled through the shop, pausing at the door to give me another wink. I stuck my tongue out at him making him chuckle as he walked through the door. As he left I looked around the shop, sighing when I realized it was empty finally. I slipped off the stool at the register and crossed the room, flinging open the front door before I could lose my nerve.

"Are you a halfway decent baker?" I hurled the question across the street, shouting at my mother.

My question surprised her. She sat there, book in hand, staring at me, just blinking.

"Well, are you? Because I need a hand with the bakery. I figure you've got a stake in seeing it do well or you wouldn't be stalking the place. So what do you say?"

She looked away, finding her bookmark on the bench, taking care to mark her place and then closing the book. "Yes, I'm a halfway decent baker. I can also run the register, make coffee, and lots of other things."

"Good. You've got a job." I turned and went back inside, rushing to help the customers who'd slipped in during the few seconds we'd been talking.

As I rung up the two women I watched her gather her things, tucking her book into her big purse, adding the snacks she'd had spread out beside her. When she came into the bakery it was with slow, timid steps. She looked around with wide eyes and I realized as odd as it had been for me to come to this place it must have been doubly so for her. I was a stranger to the bakery. She'd had a lifetime here. I was surprised when tears filled her eyes as she walked around the room. When she finally came over to the display cases a few silent tears had slipped down her cheeks. I felt the irritation in me crack a bit. Like ice on a sunny winter day, crack after crack danced through it, weakening the wall I'd put up between us. I smiled at her.

"How can I help, kiddo?"

"Well, first off, never call me 'kiddo' again. Second, there are cookies in the oven. They should be about ready to come out. Can you take care of them?"

She nodded, slipping behind the counter.

"There's a very large cat staring at me." I looked over my shoulder, not surprised to see BC sitting on one of the stools at the work counter.

"Meet BC the Bakery Cat." He watched me closely while I spoke, the tip of his tail twitching. "BC, you know the rules. Out of the kitchen."

He meowed and I glared at him. He'd had enough oven mitts and towels thrown at him to know better than to stay when I'd told

62

him to leave. He hopped off the stool and stalked out of the kitchen, probably to wait beside the side door for one of Mallie's crew to let him out. I reminded myself again to ask Mallie to put a pet door in for BC.

"You have a very unusual cat."

I smiled, thanking a customer then looked back at Mom. "You have no idea. I'm pretty sure he can open doors. I know I put him outside a couple of hours ago."

We worked the rest of the day side-by-side in almost complete silence, only speaking when we had to. There were too many things unsaid between us for causal conversation. After running into each other a few times we developed a rhythm. It soon became clear where each of us worked the best. Mom was much better with the people and running the register so she stayed close to the front, stepping into the role of baking assistant without complaint. I took point on all the baking, moving through my normal things with more speed than I was used to. It made a huge difference to have someone running the register and keeping the cases full. I wasn't racing back and forth all day. I even had time toward the end of the day to make several batches of cookies, leaving them in the big fridge on their cookie sheets, ready to go right into the oven the next day. By the time we closed up at four I was almost caught up and ready for tomorrow. Dough needing to rise overnight was sitting on the proofing rack next to the office door. I set an alarm on my phone so I wouldn't forget to come get the bread into the oven at the right time.

As Mom cleaned up the front of the shop I cleaned the kitchen. By the time Mallie's crew came pounding down the stairs at five the shop was shut up and ready for the next day. For the first time since I'd opened I wasn't ending the day so tired I could hardly move.

"Thank you. It is nice to not be dead on my feet. Maybe now I can run to the store and get some groceries. I'll see you tomorrow?"

"Sure thing, kid... Joy."

"Good. I start baking at six o'clock. Try to be here by then please."

She slipped out the front door, heading to the beat up little car she'd shown up in every day. I locked up the shop behind her, watching her drive away. BC padded up behind me, big furry feet almost silent on the wood floors. I'd given up trying to keep him out of the front of the shop. If I could just claim the kitchen as a cat free zone I'd be happy. I looked down when he leaned against my leg, begging for attention. Dropping to the floor I pulled him into my lap. After wiggling and trying to bite me several times he flipped onto his back and closed his eyes as I rubbed his belly. I stared down at him, wondering for the third or fourth time what kind of cat he was. I'd thought he was a fully-grown cat when I'd found him but after being on regular meals he'd continued growing and growing. He was getting huge.

I looked around the empty shop, looking at it without the haze of exhaustion for the first time since I'd opened. I started to think about doing more than just running the shop. The walls were bare. They could use some art. Or a mural or something. If I hired more help I could free up enough time to do something. BC meowed and drew my attention off the walls. He jumped up and headed toward the stairs. I knew what he wanted -- food. My stomach growled and I realized I was hungry too. As I followed him upstairs I decided it had been a good day. I'd gotten along with my mother but avoided the big conversation I wasn't ready to have. Baby steps toward something better. Like I'd told Will and Mallie, I forgave her. I didn't trust her though. I didn't trust her to stay. I couldn't bring myself to let her close. I didn't know if I would survive her abandoning me again.

Chapter Fifteen

I stood in the doorway of the tiny office off the kitchen, papers flooding the space, filling the earth-toned room with a snowy white mess of invoices, receipts, and more.

"Um. Will. What did you do to my office?"

Will looked up at me from the ancient computer and glared at me.

"Whoa. What did I do?"

He sighed, looking around at the mess before zeroing back in on me.

"You're terrible at this."

"At what?" I stepped cautiously through the stacks of invoices, receipts, and more to claim the other chair. The big desk and the boxy out-of-date computer sitting on it overwhelmed the office. A long, low file cabinet set across from the desk. It forced anyone who wanted to sit and work to slip between the two obstacles with a cautious side-step. Behind the second chair sat a cheap metal bookcase scattered with binders, ledgers, and recipe books. It was a staggering amount of stuff for a room no bigger than eight by eight feet. Will's snowstorm of paper compressed the space even more.

"This. All of this." He pointed at the piles of paper, the ledger on the desk, and even the old computer. "You are a genius baker but you're a terrible business woman. You keep terrible records. You have zero organization."

"Don't hold anything back there Will." He wasn't telling me anything I didn't already know. I knew the things I did well and business related work wasn't anywhere on that list.

He glared at me again then turned back to the computer.

"I never claimed anything other than a baker. I've never done the business thing. I've always been the chick in the kitchen." I knew I needed to do more research on proper pricing. I just didn't know where to start. Like Will said, I was not a business woman.

He huffed in frustration and took a deep breath, no doubt winding up to lecture me about my poor bookkeeping habits or something else dry and boring. Thankfully Mallie appeared in the doorway, distracting Will before he could speak.

"Woah. Did one of the file cabinets explode?"

"No, Will did. Apparently my lack of business savviness created this."

"Ah. Well, Will thinks most people lack business savvy. He does the books for Dad and I, too, for that very reason."

"She makes you look like a numbers savant, Mal. She's... she's..."

"Hopeless?" I supplied the word with a laugh clinging to my voice.

"Well, before you guys get into an argument about how awful you are at all things business, I wanted to let you know I've got the windows above the interior doors in upstairs. Those transoms look great and really brighten up the bedrooms. The sky lights will go in tomorrow."

"Wonderful. The kitchen?"

"Lower cabinets are in. Uppers will go up tomorrow. It sort of helped to start with everything so trashed. We'll be painting and cleaning it all up in no time." She vanished as fast as she'd appeared, eager to avoid even being adjacent to the lecture on business I was about to get.

I heard the bell over the front door tinkle and stepped away from the office so I could see the front door. My last customer of the day had paused in the door, calling thank you as she disappeared into the evening. It had been a busy Friday. I was glad to be done for the day. Mom walked to the door, locking it up and starting to clean up the tables. She glanced my way, a question on her face. I knew she'd heard Will start to lecture me. I waved her off, letting her know I had things, hoping she'd head back to the hotel she'd mentioned. I knew there was still prep work for tomorrow to be done. A kitchen to clean, too. I didn't want her to get drug into this though. I still wasn't comfortable letting her too far into my world. Mom finished lowering the blinds then grabbed her purse, heading out the side door, waving goodbye. As I turned back to Will I caught a quick change on his face. He was still wearing his frustration with me but there was something else there. Something I couldn't understand. Something running deeper than simple frustration with a friend. Before I could puzzle it out it was gone and he started to rant at me about the importance of keeping detailed records. He used a vocabulary foreign to me. Terms like "cost of sales," "net profit," and "break-even point."

"I have no idea what you're talking about, Will."

He rolled his eyes at me, telling me it was obvious to him I didn't understand.

"How about I make us something to eat and you start at the beginning?"

"Food would be good." As I waded through the mess to the door he started to tidy the papers he'd strung out across the room. He looked like a school teacher preparing for a lesson. I shuddered, fighting the urge to run. I'd always hated school. Learning was great fun, lessons, not so much.

*****

"Okay, so you've got to factor in the opportunity cost to your prices. So let's look at one of the recipes you're selling and see how much it costs to make it. Then we can figure out the cost per serving. Then we can figure out the price."

I stared across the desk at Will while my brain struggled to process what he'd just said. He made it sound so simple and easy. I looked over at the plate that had once held a stack of cookies. I tried to wish some more onto the plate but it didn't work.

"Will. You seem to have forgotten you're talking to someone who never finished high school."

"So. You got your GED later, didn't you?"

I shook my head *no* and looked away from him. I regretted not getting it. Now I felt too old to go back and finish my high school level education.

"Seriously?"

"Yes. I know it doesn't make much sense to you, fancy college guy, but no, I never did. I was in a group home at the end of high school. I was a poor student so when people stopped making me go to school I stopped going. I've been working two or three jobs at a time just to pay rent and put gas in my truck since I was eighteen. Getting my stupid GED or going to college has always been the furthest thing from my mind. Not everyone is cut out for school. Not everyone is smart enough for it."

He stared hard at me, his eyes narrowed as he focused and thought. The attention made me want to squirm in my seat or get up and walk around. Anything to get those intense eyes off me. I forced myself to stay still though and hold his gaze.

"You didn't do that bad in school, if I remember right."

"What? How would you know? Did you get my records or something?" When I glared at him he looked away and I knew he had. "Was getting my school transcripts a necessary part of tracking me down? We were in very different worlds in high school, Will. A kid with a family and a kid on their own..."

"It couldn't have been very different. School is school."

"No it's not. Kids are ruthless. If you show up wearing second hand clothes, shoes with holes, and a plastic grocery bag instead of a backpack. You don't have any idea how isolating it can be. I was invisible. To the other kids. To the teachers. I was miserable and being miserable doesn't make going to school very much fun."

Will looked away just as I did, my frankness making us both uncomfortable. Out in the kitchen a timer started to buzz and I jumped up, fleeing into the other room. I opened one of the ovens and took out a tray of sourdough rolls I'd stuffed with pepperoni and pizza sauce. I sprinkled shredded cheese over the rolls and set them back in the oven for a few more seconds, grabbing two plates from a nearby stack while the cheese melted.

"Those smell amazing." I looked over my shoulder, not surprised the smell of dinner had drawn Will out of the office. I smiled, proud of myself and happy I'd impressed him.

"Come on. Eat." I sat the two plates on the white marble top of the working counter, pulling up one of the two high stools, sitting down to eat my share of the food. Will took the other stool and we ate in silence until not even a crumb was left. We'd been going over the books for what felt like days. I knew it had just been a few hours but my brain was fried. Will had kept up a steady lecture the whole time, even following me around the kitchen while I'd whipped up a quick dinner for us.

"You weren't kidding. You do know how to bake," he said as he popped the last bite of roll into his mouth.

"This is my world, Will." I flung out my arms, gesturing to the room. "A kitchen is the one place in the world where I don't screw up everything I touch. It is the one place where I'm the A student. It is the one place where I am good at anything." I stood, gathering our empty plates.

"I'm sure you're good at more things than you realize. Not finishing school doesn't mean anything. You're not stupid."

"Thanks. I know I'm not."

He studied me again, his eyes narrowing again. I named it his thinking face and turned away to hide a smile.

"You're not stupid, Joy."

His statement stopped my journey to the pair of sinks across from the stoves. I sat our dishes down, turning back to him. I couldn't reply. I told myself I knew I wasn't stupid. The lost kid I'd been was still worried she was. I hadn't told Will the whole truth. I hadn't stopped going to school simply because I wasn't being forced. It was also because of the teachers. Teacher after teacher had written me off. I was too much trouble. I was too inconsistent. I was too stubborn. I was too stupid. The things they'd said had haunted me.

"So what's an opportunity cost again?" I turned our conversation back to business and far away from my past.

Chapter Sixteen

When the box with the bright purple label showed up, I forgot everything else going on in the bakery. Mom checking out customers. BC sneaking back into the kitchen for the third time today. Everything faded into the background. The small box with the purple label was a treasure I'd been waiting for. In it was dried, culinary lavender for Mallie's wedding cake. I tugged a paring knife out of my pocket, cutting open the box. Inside were four jars, nestled in shredded lavender paper, filled to the top with tiny lavender flowers. More than I'd need for Mallie's cake but I hoped the wedding would give the city residents a taste for lavender. I had an idea for a honey lavender bread I was dying to try.

One of the ovens started to buzz so I put the box to the side, pausing for a split second to open a jar and take a deep whiff. It was one of the most intoxicating scents in the world. I wanted to make certain Mallie had it all around her on her special day. It had been her mother's favorite scent, she'd explained. I wanted to be sure there was some part of her mom there for her. I just hoped I could create something delicious with the lavender flowers.

"Joy! The cookies!"

Mom's shout snapped me out of my head, the smell of burning cookies making me run into the kitchen, the lavender in the storeroom forgotten. It was too late though. When I opened the oven black smoke billowed out. Three trays of cookies, all burnt into coal.

"Damn, damn, damn." It was all I could say. I got distracted thinking about cake ideas and ruined the cookies. Since getting a lesson on the business side of the bakery all I could see were dollar signs as I threw out the cookies.

"We need more help." Mom appeared beside me, holding out a hand for one of the cookie sheets. "I'll try to save this once they cool. I think it's time to hang up the sign, honey."

We both looked at the *Help Wanted* sign. It had been sitting leaning against the cooling racks since Will had not so subtly brought it by two days ago. It had been hard enough to hire Mom. I didn't like being dependent on people. I was starting to realize though there was no way for me to run this bakery without depending on people. Being a baker had allowed me to be a one woman show. Being a business owner was forcing me to give it up.

"Okay. I give. We can't do this alone." I snatched the sign and stomped through the bakery past customers, propping the sign up in one of the front windows. "You guys, spread the word," I said to the people scattered around the shop. "Abbott Bakery is hiring."

*****

There was a young woman standing among the empty tables holding the Help Wanted sign I'd stuck in the window earlier in the day. Her red hair, just a shade darker than my own, was wet from the rain that had started to fall a bit ago. I was glad I had sent Mom back to her hotel for the day when it had started to thunder. I remembered how much trouble she'd always had driving on slick roads. When we'd been on the road and hit a storm she would just pull over and wait it out. Slick roads had terrified her. So I'd sent her packing at the first clap of thunder and closed up the shop myself and apparently forgot to lock the front door.

"I'm closed for the day," I said, sliding the back of the display case closed and setting the tray of unsold bread on the counter. I waited for the girl to speak but she stayed silent.

"Can I help you?" I asked, a little irritated by her quiet stare.

She held the sign out toward me.

"You're going to have to learn to speak to people if you want to work here."

The girl swallowed hard, cleared her throat and spoke. "I'm here about the job. Ma'am."

"Okay. Can you bake?"

"A little. My gran used to let me help her."

"Can you take direction in a kitchen? Follow a recipe? Run a cash register? That sort of thing?"

"Yes, ma'am."

I looked her up and down, wondering why in the world I felt like I should hire this kid. I didn't know if this place could handle three red-heads in it. Although she didn't seem like much trouble. Quiet little mouse.

"Okay. Come on then. Let's see what you can do." I turned and headed back to the kitchen. Behind me I heard her set down the sign and follow me.

"What's your name, kid?"

"Lane and I'm twenty-three. I'm not a kid, ma'am."

"Okay then. Not a kid. Got it. Stop calling me ma'am. It's Joy. Just Joy." I walked through the kitchen to the office, grabbing a binder of recipes. It was one of my own. I'd dragged it from job to job for years, adding to it as I discovered new recipes. I planned to make one with all the recipes my grandfather had tucked into cookbooks and shoeboxes but hadn't been able to spare the time yet.

I laid the binder in front of Lane, flipping it open and turning pages until I found something I thought would challenge her but not overwhelm her. Oatmeal cookies. Not too hard but not too easy. A misstep could tank the cookies. A natural instinct for baking could make them amazing though. Whenever I made them just for me I swapped the oil for applesauce and added flaxseed and dark chocolate chips. It made the tasty cookie something even tastier and a lot healthier. Which made them guilt free too. I wondered what she would do with them. I opened the binder's rings and pulled out the wrinkled and stained recipe.

"Here's your interview. Make these. You can take it with you or just stay here and use the kitchen. I've got some work to do in the office so I'll be right here."

"That's it? No interview or references?"

"You want to work in a bakery, you better be able to bake. This is your interview and the result will be your references." Lane took the paper from me and stared at it. I watched as she read it, pleased when I saw a spark of confidence shine in her eyes. She folded it and tucked it inside her coat.

"Okay. I'll be back."

I smiled at her. "I'll be here. Be creative. You'll get bonus points."

I walked to the swinging doors behind her, watching as she tugged her jacket tight around her and headed back out into the rain. I smiled again when I saw she'd grabbed the Help Wanted sign. Someone didn't want to take the chance I'd hire someone else. The move made me like the girl. I would have done the same thing for a job I really wanted. I hoped her cookies wouldn't be terrible. I wanted to hire her.

Chapter Seventeen

By the time the weekend rolled around I had another baking assistant. Lane had returned the next morning, bringing me a bag of some of the best oatmeal cookies I'd ever had. She'd added white chocolate chips and crunchy freeze dried strawberries. It was brilliant and I wanted to put them on the bakery menu. Lane had protested a bit, uncomfortable with my praise, but gave in, saying her Mom would be so proud of her.

She settled into a rhythm in the kitchen within an hour, working as a go-between of sorts. She helped me and helped Mom, filling in the gaps when we both got busy. Lane was some of the best help I'd ever had in the kitchen. I'd worked with dozens of different people over the years and she went right to the top of my list. She had an instinct for baking like few of my former coworkers ever had. She also came with an unusual side benefit. As it turned out, she was the sheriff's daughter. As the days passed, Sheriff Walter Dodge started stopping by every afternoon to check on his kid and have a midday snack of cookies.

He also appeared to be stopping by to make Mom uncomfortable. By the end of Lane's first full week, Mom had taken to going to the bathroom or stepping out for some air every time the brown and white cruiser pulled up in front of the shop. When Saturday drew to a close I decided it was time for our long overdue heart-to-heart conversation -- one I planned to start with the subject of the good sheriff.

"Mom, can you stick around after we close up? Talk a bit?" She paused at my question, the blinds she'd been lowering frozen halfway down the big front windows. She turned and nodded. I was nervous. I needed to know why she'd never come back for me and where she'd been. I wanted to know why things had been so bad between her and

75

her parents. Why had she hated them so much? Why had she never contacted them again? I had so many questions for her. As I remembered her vanishing earlier that day when the sheriff had stopped by, I added another question to my list. Why did she hide from Sheriff Dodge?

I tossed BC one of his catnip mice and grabbed the two mugs of hot cocoa I'd had ready, meeting her at a table in the center of the bakery. She took the mug, wrapping both hands around it, and breathing in the warm, chocolate scented steam floating like a halo. The day had turned chilly quickly, a strong cold front turning the September day into November in just a few hours. We both pulled out chairs at the same time, sitting with one leg tucked under us. I had to smile as we mirrored each other. We'd been doing it a lot since she'd come to work here. It had bothered me at first but now I kind of liked it. It was nice seeing my habits in someone else.

"What did you want to talk about, Joy Claire?" I watched her closely as she sipped her cocoa. Her hands had a little tremor, telling me she was nervous about this talk too.

I decided to just go for it. The worst that could happen was she would leave again. I'd survived it when I was twelve. I could survive it again. I visualized my list and picked a question at random. "So... what did your letter say?"

She smiled and set aside the mug, disappearing into the office and coming out with the familiar envelope. I'd told her it was in there waiting for her the day I'd hired her. I told her I didn't feel right reading it. She'd pretended to not hear me and left it sitting on the corner of the desk where I saw it every day. She sat and offered it to me but I waved it away. I couldn't read it. It would have felt like an intrusion. I would rather her just summarize it for me and told her as much.

"Your grandfather." Mom paused and took a sip of her cocoa, settling back into the chair across from me. I drank a bit of mine as she resumed speaking. "Your grandfather was a hard man. He had this set

76

of rules he felt everyone should live by. I'm sure you figured out I failed to follow those rules."

"Yeah, I put it together pretty fast."

"This will shock you but he said he was sorry. For making me feel like choosing to have you and keep you was wrong. For making me feel like I could never come home."

"He did?"

She nodded, looking away from me to the tabletop. She traced the pattern of the grain with a fingertip.

"He wanted me to marry your father. When I refused to, he told me I had to go away, stay with relatives far from Rio Verde, to hide my pregnancy and to give you up. I refused to do that too. Instead I stayed here and became the bad pregnant girl at the high school, causing general shame on the family and becoming the source of a lot of gossip. When I had you I put the plan I'd dreamed up into action. I took all the money I'd been able to scrape together and packed up my car and hit the road. Momma begged me to stay. She said she'd make Dad understand. I went anyway. You know everything from there on, I'm afraid."

"Not everything, Mom. Why did you leave me? I was twelve. I still needed my mom."

She looked away, her eyes filling with tears as an expression of shame settled over her face. She lifted her mug, taking a long sip of cocoa before beginning to speak. As our cocoa cooled, Mom told me everything that happened after the night she left me. I'd known she'd had a drug problem for a long time. It had started when I was five or six when she'd been hurt working at one of those big box stores. The back injury had come with narcotic painkillers. Painkillers she'd gotten hooked on. It didn't surprise me when she told me she'd been arrested for drug possession a few times. She spun out the rest of the story telling me everything. There were close calls with police as she sunk deeper into addiction. Finally she ran across a judge who didn't see a junky before him and sentenced her to rehab instead of jail. She told me of all the times she slipped up and about all the times she got clean only to trade one addiction for another. She kept trying, though, until she finally got clean and stayed clean. By then she was deep in southern Florida, broke and unable to get back to Las Vegas to find me. When she'd come back looking for me years and years later I'd aged out of the system and moved away. Just like I had when I'd turned eighteen, she'd searched for me but hadn't been able to find me.

"Joy, can I ask you something?"

I locked eyes with her, seeing her, the real her for once. She looked so much stronger to me now.

"Why did you leave, honey? Where did you go? I did come back for you. I was just so, so late."

"What was I supposed to do, Mom? Stay there? Spend my life waiting for you? I had nothing." My voice broke and I paused. Tears started to fill my eyes and I shut them, forcing the tears back, swallowing hard, trying to keep control. I opened my eyes and looked up her. "No family. I grew up in group homes and short term foster families. I had no reason to keep waiting for you. So I did what you'd raised me to do. I wandered."

"I'm so sorry, baby. I never meant for any of this to happen to you."

"Then why did you leave me, Mom?" I couldn't stop the tears now. They raced down my cheeks, hot rivers of pain and anger.

"Baby girl," she whispered. She rose, coming to my side of the table and reaching out to hug me. I pulled away but she ignored me, wrapping me in her arms. I tensed up but as she patted my back, I broke, a little girl again taking refuge in her mother's arms. "Not coming back for you is my greatest regret. I will always be sorry but I had to get clean. I needed to. First I had to fall all the way to the bottom, and at least I kept you away from all of it."

I smiled, pushing away my tears and then reaching into my shirt, finding the long chain I always wore. I tugged it out, finding the blue and bronze token on it.

78

"You didn't save me from anything, Mom." I held up the chip. "Two years sober back in March. I'm almost three years out from my last drink. I followed you, even though neither of us realized it."

We talked the rest of the night, sitting in the dark and empty bakery for hours. She told me about the years of addiction that had kept her from me. She tugged her own sobriety chip from her pocket, proudly telling me she'd been clean and sober for fifteen years. I told her about learning how to survive, learning how to be an adult. I told her about the long hike on the Appalachian Trail and how it had been the turning point in my life. By the time we both started to yawn more than talk Mom had agreed to move into one of the spare bedrooms in the apartment and out of the hotel. As I watched her drive away, I couldn't help but shed a few happy tears. I had my mom back. For the first time since I was a kid, I had my mom back.

Chapter Eighteen

"Why do you always make jokes about being stupid? Who made you think you were?"

I tensed at Will's question. Since the day I'd asked him to help me he had made a point to come by every evening to help me with the business side of things. Business lessons, he called them. Even today, he'd come by after Sunday lunch with his folks. We'd had the bakery to ourselves and Mom camped out upstairs watching a marathon of her favorite tv show. Today, like all the other days before, Will had taught me about the things that went into running a business. He always ended the lesson by asking me a different version of the same question. I was learning a lot but dodging the same question was wearing me thin. I had to admit though, he was right. His repeated questions had made me realize that I did cut a lot of jokes about being stupid. It was a bad habit, but it had sort of helped me over the years. I could beat people to the punch. Call myself dumb before they could.

I glanced over at him, perched on one of the stools at the work counter, and returned my focus to the dough beneath my hands. I was baking for myself today. *For Mom and me.* We needed some sandwich bread for our own meals. She'd moved in two days ago and I'd learned we were more alike than I realized. Toast and jam for breakfast and a sandwich for lunch. We loved our bread.

I pushed and pulled, buying time to think as I worked the dough. Buying time to decide if I trusted him enough to tell him the real reason I'd taken off all those years ago. I tossed the dough into a bowl and covered it with a towel, leaving it to rest and rise.

"I was never good at school. I know you've seen my transcripts and the grades aren't terrible. You can't see, though, how hard I had to work to get those not-terrible grades." I crossed to the sink, washing the flour off my hands while I chose my words. "I went into the system at twelve years old. Before then I never even went to school consistently. Mom would move us to a new place every six months or so. I read well enough, Mom is a good reader so there were always books. When I was little she would even help me with my reading during her sober stretches. In every other subject I was always behind. Usually always the oldest kid in class too. I was six or seven the first time a teacher called me stupid."

I paused, walking away, into the little office. He followed me without a word. As always, I felt the room change when he joined me. He filled the small space, making me on edge. Over the past several days I'd realized how aware I was of everything he did. I didn't like it. I shrugged off the feeling, or tried to, and claimed one of the worn chairs in the little room. The ever-present butterfly doing a backflip when Will locked eyes with me.

"If people tell you something enough times it becomes your truth. At least it did for me. It wasn't until I started trying to get sober that I started to realize they'd all been wrong. I think differently than lots of people and I didn't get the advantage of a formal education."

Will took over the other chair, scooting it closer to me. I couldn't help but notice how nice he smelled, like paper and ink -- like a businessman. My favorite scents had always been baking related, but this business scent was climbing the ranks.

"So why still make the jokes?" His question pulled me out of my head and back to the topic.

"I feel so..." I paused trying to find the right words. "Inadequate. This is overwhelming, this responsibility." I stopped a moment, the weight of it all heavy on my shoulders.

"I've never been anything more than a baker. Not even a head baker. I've only ever been in charge of myself and I've not done a great job with even that little bit of responsibility." I raised my eyes, finally talking to Will instead of the floor. "What if I fail?"

Will scooted the chair closer until our knees were touching.

I pulled away as he reached toward my face. "What are you doing?"

"You're crying."

"I am not."

"Yes," he said as he touched my cheek, "you are." He held his fingers before me, showing me the dampness he'd captured.

I rubbed my face, pushing away the traitorous tears. "Well, it means nothing. I'm fine."

"No you're not." He captured one of my hands, stilling my nervous movements. "You are not going to fail, do you hear me? I'm going to help you. You've got this."

I blinked hard, looking at his hands covering mine, our differing skin tones reminding me of coffee and cream. My emotions overwhelmed me and tears burned my eyes, running hot down my cheeks. I'd never told anyone any of those things. I didn't pull away when Will reached out to me a second time. Instead I let him fold me into his arms, giving me something to hang on to, his strength ebbing into me until I felt like something new was taking hold. Maybe I did have this. Maybe I wasn't going to fail. Because I had someone helping me for once. Because I had him.

"Thank you, Will. I'm not good at accepting help." I spoke into his shoulder, not quite ready to pull away from him.

"I've noticed," he said with a laugh, breaking the hug as he straightened.

As I smiled at him, Will leaned back and looked at me, his face serious. He reached out, touching my cheek. With his thumb he brushed away a stray tear, his touch feather light, his smile gentle. It said I was safe with him. It said he wasn't going anywhere. When he touched my lips with his I knew no matter what might come in the future I had something worth staying put for finally.

*****

The insistent ring of my cell phone broke the moment with Will. It had been Mallie, reminding me she and Luz were waiting for me across the square. Our long overdue girls night out. So instead of moving forward with whatever the kiss had started we went our separate ways -- Will heading home while I crossed the square and headed out with my new friends. Luz's sister Isabel joined us as we piled into Luz's little car, heading to a restaurant on the edge of town they promised me I was going to love. A place called Dot's.

They'd been right. By the time all of our food was gone and four slices of homemade buttermilk pie had appeared I was a Dot's fan for life. I was sold on these three women, too. We'd talked about everything as we'd pigged out. Luz and Mateo's house they were slowly remodeling on their own. Mallie and Tres' upcoming wedding. Isabel's growing side business decorating houses. How the bakery was doing. There was one thing I wanted to talk to them about.

"Mallie, what is the deal with your cousin?" I tossed the question out as I paused between bites of pie.

"What do you mean?" She grinned at me, a twinkle in her eyes telling me she was pretending she didn't know where I was headed with my question.

"I think she means what's the deal with Will, Mal," Luz chimed in, speaking around a mouthful of pie.

"No," Isabel added, "I think she means, is Will seeing anyone."

I flushed at Isabel's addition to my question. Isabel had hit the nail on the head.

"Ah. Yeah. I'm pretty sure all he's seeing is you, Joy."

I flushed again, making all three of my friends laugh. It was still all new to me, this group of friends thing. I saw them almost every day and always looked forward to it. Mallie stopping by to steal cookies before going to work on the apartment. Isabel dropping off things for the apartment. Luz coming over with food for Mom and me when she'd noticed us working all day without a break. Every day I got a little bit of time with at least one of them. I'd never had problems making friends, but I'd always had trouble keeping them. Yet these three, I knew I'd be friends with them forever and I didn't do forever. It was amazing to me how fast we'd formed a tight bond. I felt lucky and blessed and wondered if this would be something Mallie would call a God thing.

"I always thought Will was handsome," Luz said.

"No, you didn't. Pretty sure you've called him an ass more than once."

"Only before y'all fixed things. Now he's a good guy and kind of handsome."

"I had a crush on him when I was a kid," Isabel declared.

"You did not. You would have told me."

"Hate to break it to you sister, but I don't tell you everything."

The sisters glared at each other for a half a second, then started to talk over each other in Spanish.

"This is how they fight. Give them a few minutes and they'll laugh again and be fine," Mallie said, leaning over to speak just to me. "Why'd you ask about Will, Joy? What's up?"

"Well. Umm." I looked down at the table, balling up my napkin. "Well, you see... like maybe five seconds before you called me tonight, he kissed me."

"Shut the front door." Mallie's exclamation got Luz and Isabel's attention, stopping their disagreement.

"What?" They spoke in unison, drawing a look of annoyance from Mallie.

"Will kissed Joy."

"Oh, seriously?"

"Spill it, Joy," Luz demanded.

As the restaurant closed down I backtracked, telling them about the conversations which had led up to my talk with Will a few hours earlier. Their questions derailed the story over and over again but I didn't mind. It was good to open up to them. It was better than good. It was freeing to share my stories with them. I remembered something I'd read in the old Bible the night before. Each night I'd picked it up, choosing one of the many underlined verses and looking it up on a Bible study website. It was just a simple verse in chapter four of Ecclesiastes, verses nine and ten. It talked about how it was better to be two than to be alone because if you fell, you would be supported by the other. As I left the now closed restaurant I knew I'd found my people. These women would never let me fall and now, I knew, neither would Will. Even when I moved on when the year was up, I knew I'd always have this tribe of people I'd found.

Chapter Nineteen

Mornings were my favorite time of day. Not the watching the sun come up kind of mornings. The being up and about before the sun, before the city, before anyone woke. Then, it was like I was the only one in the world. Since the day Mom had moved in I'd been able to get back to one of my favorite morning pastimes, jogging. With her starting the day's baking I could slip away for a good run. I'd been picking streets at random each day jogging my way through the residential areas that spun out from the city center.

Today though I followed a familiar route. I'd picked the street one day simply because it had pretty trees in all the front yards. It was peaceful under the shady branches. I'd noticed Will's car parked beside a tidy old house the same morning and had been ending my jog on the street ever since. Today I was hoping to catch him up. It had been a busy week and I hadn't seen him since the night he kissed me. He'd texted, postponing our business lessons so he could put in extra hours at the bank on something for a big customer. I'd missed him.

I turned into the quiet, tree-lined road, dropping down to a walk. I wanted to enjoy the pretty street. The short road looped back toward downtown and was full of older, small houses. The first day I'd found it I realized it was the perfect cool down street. I could relax, catch my breath, and imagine what life would be like in this little oasis of a road. Several of the front yards held collections of colorful plastic toys or child-sized bicycles so I knew the peace was just an early in the morning thing. After half a block I reached Will's house and tugged my cell phone free from my sweatpants. The house was flooded with light, the first one awake in the degrading darkness. In a big window I could see his treadmill with an empty water bottle sitting on it. I knew he'd been up running just like I had. As I pulled up his name and pressed dial I decided it was time to invite him to run outside with me.

"You should start running with me each morning."

"Who is this?" It had become his normal greeting when I called him. No matter what time of day, even if he could see me calling him, he always pretended to not know who I was. It made me smile every time.

"It's Joy. I'm stalking you. Look out your front window."

He appeared at the window, waving hello when he saw me standing out front. I made faces at him, making him laugh. "Creeper. What do you want this early in the morning?"

"Come walk with me."

"I just finished running. I need to shower and get ready for work." I could hear him walking through the house as he spoke and headed toward the front door, guessing he was headed there too.

"No. You need to come cool down with me," I said as he unlocked the door and smiled at me.

"Only if you'll let me treat you to breakfast."

"I will never turn down food." He ducked back into the house, returning with a set of keys and a handful of cash.

We set off side-by-side down the wide sidewalk. I shot a glance over at Will, noting how different post work out Will was when compared to just off work Will. In knee length running shorts and a faded Rio Verde High sweatshirt, he was free from pressed slacks and dress shirts for once. In fact, his round, wire frame glasses were the one thing still the same.

"I like this version of you best," I said, breaking the comfortable silence.

"Sweaty and probably smelly?"

"Well," I paused and leaned over, pretending to smell him, "I didn't want to say anything but..."

He laughed and gave me a gentle shove into the empty street. "You aren't exactly rosy yourself there, Joy. So how far did you run this morning?"

"Not too far. Around four miles. I needed to think."

"You're out here every day?"

"Now that Mom is helping out, yeah. She starts up things at the bakery while I run. I'd been taking a different route each day but I found your street, now it's my way home. So yeah, every day, I run. How else can I bake -- and eat -- all day and not weigh a ton?"

"I should start coming with you."

"Told you."

We walked in silence for a block, enjoying the slowly waking city. The sun was just starting to lighten the sky, turning the inky black to soft gray. I knew soon splashes of color would appear in the sky followed by a special, dusty blue I'd learned to associate with Texas skies.

"So why'd you decide to give me a call this morning? Do you want to talk about the other night?"

"The way I dumped my whole, sad story on you?"

"Or the kiss."

I flinched when he brought up the one thing I'd been hoping to ignore. The kiss. It had hovered in the back of my head since it happened. I wanted him to kiss me again. The lonely kid I'd been was doing cartwheels inside me. She was thrilled. She was falling fast. Another part of me, a big part of me, was scared. It kept telling me to run. It kept telling me if I wasn't careful that lonely kid was going to take charge and try to stay here once my grandfather's required year was up.

"Yeah. It can't happen again."

"Oh really. I can't wait to hear why."

I looked over and he was watching me intently, equal parts amusement and irritation on his face. I looked away and launched my planned speech. "It can't happen again because I'm not staying here. When the year is up I'm gone. I don't do permanent. I've never been good at it. I move around. I go where the wind blows. I'm not good at anything else."

I braved a look over and this time he looked away before I could read his expression.

"Very interesting. It sounds like a lonely way to live."

"I'm good with it. I get to reinvent myself with each town. I get to see the world. What more do I need?"

"Friends. Family. A support system."

"I've got friends. I make friends everywhere I go. Family... well family is still something I'm not sure about."

"A support system," he repeated.

"I'm my own support system."

He glanced over, eyes narrowed. I was getting on his nerves, I knew.

"Fine. People you can lean on, count on, depend on. People who love you for who you are, who you truly are."

I was quiet for a few steps, thinking about the kind of ties he was talking about. They scared me. Those deep connections with people rang warning bells in my head. They felt like chains to me. Anchors. Traps. I'd thought I could get used to them but our kiss had set off something in me. Now all I could hear was an old, familiar voice in my head telling me to run.

"I'm fine on my own."

"Okay then. We won't talk about the kiss, but you can't stop me from thinking about it."

"Please don't. I'm just not good at this kind of thing, Will. Think about someone better suited for you."

"Not good at what kind of thing?"

"Relationship stuff. Guy girl things. It makes me want to run. It makes me feel trapped."

"You're not trapped here."

"Aren't I? By my grandfather's will?"

"That's not meant to be a trap. Think of it as an opportunity. An opportunity to build something. Something you will want to stick around for."

"Nothing has ever made me want to stick around for very long."

He laughed, looking over at me with a smile on his face. "I'll accept that challenge, Joy. I'm pretty sure that, if you'll let me, I can make you want to stick around for a long time. Maybe even for a lifetime. With me."

I must have looked as terrified as I felt because he burst out laughing and kept laughing until we sat down for breakfast on a bench beside a tiny burrito stand I'd somehow missed each morning. Once we'd eaten and I'd told him to shut up several times I brought up the real reason I'd wanted to talk to him.

At dinner with the girls, I'd learned Luz and Teo were struggling. With bills. With the renovation of their house. With a lot of the things I was sure newly married people faced. Luz fed me at least three meals a week, always free. Sometimes she'd stick around and visit. She'd never come right out and said it, but I'd put the pieces together. Their house was their biggest problem. They'd gotten a deal on a foreclosure and were learning why. As they fixed cosmetic problems they were finding bigger problems. It was overwhelming her and Mateo and I wanted to help. I couldn't take away their bills but I could reach out to some of my new friends and they could reach out to their friends. Maybe together we could see about fixing up the house. I'd watched enough home improvement shows to know a small army of people could do amazing things. I was hoping Will could help me gather the necessary army. I laid out my idea for Will as we walked back toward his house.

"I know they won't take money so a fundraiser won't work but if we can fix up the house..." I trailed off watching Will take in my crazy plan.

"I think it's brilliant," he said at last, catching me off guard with a one armed hug and a quick kiss on the forehead.

"Quit it." I shoved him away, pointing at him. "I said no. Not happening. I'm leaving in a year. No ties."

"Sure. Whatever you say, Miss I-Just-Made-A-Plan-To-Help-My-New-Friend."

I rolled my eyes at him and waved goodbye as he turned up the driveway to his house. I shook my head at his behavior the whole way home, puzzling over this man I barely knew. The butterfly in my stomach did acrobatics as I thought -- warning me there might just be some truth to Will's assurance that I'd marry him one day.

*****

When I got back to the bakery the center of town was waking up. The sun had climbed high enough to tint the sky with shades of pink and orange. Across the square, The RWB was opening for business, the scents of their famous oatmeal perfumed the air. I stopped at the side door, watching cars pass by with yawning drivers. The owner of the coffee shop across the street called good morning as she opened up for the day. I knew soon the smell of her coffee would join The RWB's oatmeal. I pushed open the door, following BC as he darted in too then trotted into the kitchen. I followed him in and scooped him up then dropped him back out in the hallway.

"No cats in the kitchen, mister."

I smiled when I heard Mom open an oven. The first loaves of the day. I knew we were adding another scent to the perfume of the square -- fresh bread. Before long we'd add the sweet scent of cookies, muffins, and more.

"Did you have a good run?"

I didn't answer right away, instead pulling a bottle of water out of the big industrial fridge and taking a long drink. "I did. I ran into Will and he bought me breakfast."

"Oh yeah? You know, I sure do see a lot of Will around here."

"Well he does work next door and he is the boss of the will. He has to keep an eye on things."

"Kid, I'm pretty sure that young man isn't keeping an eye on things. He's keeping an eye on you."

My face warmed instantly. My embarrassment trumped my annoyance at being called a kid. I was sure I'd gone as red as my hair so I turned away, heading out of the kitchen, muttering words like shower and whatever as my mom laughed behind me. As I got ready for the day, I wondered if this was what having a good relationship

91

with your mom was like. Teasing and laughing. It was so strange. Yet something else too. Nice. We still needed to talk about things but for now, it was nice to have her here, acting like a mom. I promised myself today I'd corner her for another mother/daughter talk. I still wanted to know why she vanished every time the sheriff came by. Or why she never mentioned her mom. I had a list somewhere of things to ask her about.

Of course nothing has ever gone the way I planned in my life so I wasn't too surprised when the day went off the rails. We were slammed from almost the moment I unlocked the front door. Two women came in to order cookies for birthday parties. A secretary from the city offices down the road came and bought every one of our miniature loaves of sourdough so she could make sandwiches for a lunch meeting. Mom, Lane, and I raced from the kitchen to the cash register over and over all day. We couldn't keep the cases stocked. By the time we closed at five it was officially the best day the bakery had had since reopening.

The three of us cleaned up, Lane heading home and Mom heading to the grocery store. I barely registered the chime of the front door, as I worked in the office, getting the evening deposit ready like Will had taught me to. I wondered, for a moment if Mom was already back, but a quick glance at the clock told me she'd just been gone twenty minutes. When I heard the creak of the little half door blocking off the working area behind the counter I looked up, realizing someone had come into the shop. For a second I hoped it was Will but when no one spoke I knew it wasn't.

"I'm sorry, we're already closed for the day." I called out to the late comer as I came out of the office. As I walked past the side door leading into the hallway I noticed movement out of the corner of my eye and turned to look. Before I could even take a step toward the hall everything went crazy.

A man appeared in the kitchen, a crowbar in his hand. The figure I'd caught a glimpse of in the hallway charged through the swinging doors, knocking me to the ground. When he knelt over me I swung at him, connecting with his jaw. The impact shuddered down my arm and caught him off guard. I scrambled up, scanning for something to swing at him and his friend who was advancing on me, the crowbar raised and ready to swing. I backed away, away from any handy knives or pans and toward the storeroom. The one I'd punched darted closer, fists raised, a quick punch catching me on the chin and making me see stars. I swung at him out of instinct. Years of fights over food and clothes in rough group homes had taught me well. I caught him again, right in the nose, sending him staggering backward as blood poured from his now broken nose. Before I had time to react his friend swung the crowbar, catching me on the arm. I heard the bone break but swung at him with my other fist, missing as the pain hit me and made me stagger back. The other man stepped forward, putting his full weight into his punch as he caught me on the temple. I saw his other fist coming as the world went dark and the floor raced up toward me.

Chapter Twenty

I woke up slowly, in little slices of time. Seconds at first. Then minutes. Nothing made any sense. The bits of time gave me pieces of information which didn't add up right away. Unfamiliar voices. A bed too narrow to be my own with stiff sheets and an odd sensation of being too high off the ground. The clothes on me weren't mine either. Things were attached to me, things that tangled in my hands. Strange hands touched me and strange sounds surrounded me. Finally a familiar voice broke through the thick, stiff fog clinging to me. My mom's voice. She said my name, once then twice, just a whisper followed by prayers. As I clung to her voice, pulling myself free, I wondered why she was praying.

"Mom..."

The single word was as all it took to set off chaos. Such a small word for such a huge reaction. As my mother and then the hospital room came into focus people in scrubs came into the room. Through the blur of motion and noise they created, I kept my gaze fixed on Mom. She'd pulled me free of the white, timeless fog I'd been in. She was the anchor holding me there. Finally, when just a doctor and her were left I looked away and tried my voice again.

"What happened?"

The doctor smiled, a kind smile, and turned to Mom, allowing her to explain. Though nothing she said rang a bell, I believed her when she told me the bakery had been robbed. As I shifted in the narrow bed, my body protesting each movement, I believed her when she told me I'd put up a fight and gotten myself a beating in return. It explained the cast on my arm and what I thought must be a bandage on my head though it was nothing more than a white blur at the corner of my left eye.

"BC?" My voice was squeaky and half strength. I took a deep breath, wincing when stabbing pain made me realize I must have some broken ribs too.

"Trust you to worry about the cat. You always were an animal lover. He was upstairs in the apartment. They never knew he was there." Mom kept talking, telling me the office had been trashed and all of the day's earnings as well as the cash I kept on hand to tip delivery drivers was gone. They'd broken all of the glass display cases just for spite. No one had seen a thing. They slipped out the loading dock, vanishing into the evening. Mallie's crew had been long gone. Most of the businesses on the square had been closed other than the few restaurants who'd been packed. They'd timed it right for the time people would be least likely to notice something going on in the bakery.

I tried to process everything she told me but the white, timeless place pulled at me, drawing me back down into a world where nothing but sleep and disjointed time existed.

When I woke the second time Mom was asleep in a chair beside a window I didn't remember from when I awake earlier. Outside I could see gray clouds and rain slipping down the glass but nothing else. On the other side of my bed I was surprised to find Mallie watching me with a smile.

"Hey, Joy. How you feeling?"

I was careful to breathe shallow as I gathered myself to answer her, the memory of the broken ribs and the pain they caused vivid even though the white fog was still trying to control my brain.

"Like someone beat the crap out of me. How do I look?"

"Ravishing." A laugh was on her words so I knew I must look as good as I felt.

"How long have I been in here?"

Her smile faded a bit. "Two days. Almost three."

I stared at her, struggling to understand what she was saying. I didn't understand how I'd lost almost three days.

"They messed you up, Joy. I guess you fought pretty hard. The sheriff thinks it was the blow to the head that took you down." I touched my head as she spoke, cautiously pressing the bandage, closing my eyes when my touch made pain ricochet through my head. "Careful. There's ten stitches under there."

"What about the bakery, Mallie?"

"The bakery is fine. It's closed right now. Will's got BC over at his house. The sheriff won't let any of us over there until they've processed everything."

"I miss him."

"Will or BC?" The laugh was back in her voice. I smiled at her and struggled to stay with her as the void started to pull me away again. I fought but soon the familiar white nothingness drug me down into sleep again.

The third time I pulled free I knew I would be able to stay awake. Instead of slowly coming awake I woke in an instant. So fast in fact that I wondered for a second if an alarm had gone off. For a few seconds it was as if I'd been woken by my usual, five am alarm sounding off on my cell phone. As the hospital room came into focus reality took back over. This time I found Will asleep in the chair beside the window. Outside the gray clouds and rain had been replaced by the inky black of the sky, the dimly lit room allowing me to see a few stars but no moon or any buildings. I took in the whole room, looking it over carefully, committing it all to memory, making it real in my foggy brain. In the corner near Will, mounted on the wall was a TV. It was on but muted, a show I didn't recognize playing out on the screen. On the wall across from the bed was a big dry erase board. My name was on it along with the names of the nurses and doctors caring for me. I followed a beam of light to an open door. From my bed I couldn't see beyond the edge of the doorframe but I could hear hushed voices as people went on about their work. I scanned back beside the bed, finding Mom dozing in the chair where Mallie had been the last time I'd woken.

I watched her for a few minutes, remembering I'd wanted to talk to her. I'd wanted to pull out my list of questions and grill her. None of it felt so important from the hospital bed. She had stayed. It had gotten rough and ugly and scary and she'd stayed.

"I love you, Mom."

"You too, kiddo." She muttered the words, still mostly asleep. I didn't wake her. It was enough to know she'd heard me. It was enough she'd said it back. It was enough that I believed her.

Chapter Twenty-One

My second day of wakefulness started with sunshine. Bright, warm sunshine streaming in the window. My first thought was that I now understood why BC was always moving from sunbeam to sunbeam. There was something wonderfully comforting about a sunny spot by a window. I wanted to sink back into sleep and soak up the soothing warmth. The doctor who appeared in my sunbeam had other ideas though.

"Two days in a row. Awake and alert. A very good thing, Miss Abbott." As he spoke he raised the bed, forcing me to sit up. He did a quick exam, checking my reflexes and such, chatting at me as he worked and dictating notes to the nurse beside him at the same time.

"When can I leave?" I'd started asking him the day before when I'd managed to stay awake for a few hours in a row. He'd been ignoring me. I hoped this time he'd answer me.

"You stay awake all day and walk around a bit, without getting dizzy, I'll consider letting you go home with your mother tomorrow." I started to correct him and tell him the bakery apartment was just a temporary home but he was gone quickly, giving the nurse who followed instructions for my care for the rest of the day. With the two of them gone I settled back into the sunbeam, forgetting my need to redefine his definition of home. I looked around the room for the first time today. I was alone, something that hadn't happened since I'd woken up two... no three days ago. A quick scan of the room revealed my solitude was temporary. In the chair beside the window was a blanket and Mom's purse. She had to be somewhere close.

My thoughts must have called her because Mom appeared, walking into the room while talking on her cell phone. She smiled when she saw me, ending the call and coming over to hug me. It was a good, long hug and I just sank into it. When she stepped away and broke the hug I caught her hand, stopping her path to the chair.

"Sit with me, Mom," I said, scooting over to make room for her on the bed. She didn't hesitate, pausing to kick off her shoes before she hopped up beside me, putting her arm around my shoulders and tugging me up against her side.

"How you feeling, Joy-bear?"

I smiled. She hadn't called me by the nickname since I was a little girl. "I'm okay. I hurt everywhere but my head is clear. I want to go back to the apartment. Mallie's wedding is two weeks away. I need to get back into gear so I can make her cake."

"Well, we can make all of those things happen just as soon as the doc clears you to go home. We're going to need to hire some more help though. With you down to one hand..."

"I know. How are your cake decorating skills? I'm not sure I can decorate a wedding cake one handed."

She squeezed my hand, not saying a word. I knew what she was telling me though. She had my back.

"Is there glass back in the cases?"

"It should go in today."

"Has Mallie's crew been allowed to go upstairs? It sure would be nice if they could finish before her wedding."

"Don't you worry about a thing, honey. Mallie's on top of it. All your friends are pitching in to get things put back right for you."

"What about the men..." I stopped, fear coming out of nowhere and overwhelming me. I still couldn't remember what had happened. One minute I'd been calling out to an unseen person, saying the shop was closed. Next I was waking up in the hospital. When I tried to think about it -- the fear would swim in and push away even the most vague memories I had of the incident.

"They're looking for them. The sheriff will fill you in. I was just talking to him. He's on his way over to talk to you about it all."

I closed my eyes, letting the peacefulness of the moment soak into me. Sitting in a sunbeam with my mom's arm around me. It was

99

quite possibly the best thing to come from all of this mess. I had my mom back. I was a big ball of pain and a little uneasy about being alone in the bakery again but I knew I wasn't on my own for once. I had my mom back. It was worth it all to have her in my life again. Opening my eyes, I sighed. If the sheriff was coming the peacefulness was about to end.

"If the sheriff is coming, can I at least brush my teeth? Maybe wash my face?"

Mom slipped out of the bed with a smile. "I'll make it happen and I'll get them to bring you some breakfast." She was out the door before I could say thank you. She worked fast. A nurse came in right away with everything I needed to clean up a bit. She helped me to the bathroom, standing close while I cleaned myself up. I avoided the mirror as best I could. A quick glance had been sobering. I was sporting a black eye and there was a massive bruise spreading out from under the bandage on my temple. There were two little bandages across a cut on my chin. There were faint bruises across my jaw and dried blood in random places they'd missed when they'd patched me up. I wasn't vain but no woman liked looking like she's lost a boxing match.

"I know, it's hard to see," said the nurse when she saw me look away. "You're healing very fast. Trust me. I was here when you were brought in. You look worlds better already."

"Worlds better?" I asked the question as I ducked my head, splashing cold water on my face, chasing away the last dredges of the days of sleep.

"Worlds better." She sounded certain, her words honest. I told myself to believe her as I brushed my teeth and let her help me wash my hair with their strange dry shampoo. By the time she helped me back to the bed my breakfast arrived along with Luz and a change of clothes.

"How'd you know I'd want those?" I hugged her as she set down the bag.

Her answer was a quick glance at Mom. She'd called her and like the great friend she was, Luz had headed right over. She was gone just as quickly as she'd gotten there, leaving Mom and I to visit and wait for the sheriff to show up. As we waited, I wondered if the odd avoidance I'd seen in her around Sheriff Dodge would appear again today. I didn't have to wait long as he showed up almost the moment I'd started to wonder about the connection between him and Mom.

As he grilled me, asking questions I couldn't answer, I watched him and Mom. It wasn't obvious but the longer I watched the more I picked up on it. They were wildly uncomfortable around each other and were going to great pains to pretend they weren't. I made myself a mental promise -- as soon as I was out of this hospital, the sheriff and I were going to have a talk without Mom around. I was starting to get an idea I hoped Sheriff Dodge would be able to confirm for me.

Chapter Twenty-Two

It was late the next day before I left the hospital. I was weak as wet toilet paper when they wheeled me out to Mom's waiting car. Scaling the stairs to the apartment required multiple breaks. Both Mom and Will chastised me for refusing to stay somewhere without stairs. Mallie's dad had offered me a place at their house, offering to turn the den into a bedroom for me. Tres and Luz's parents had offered me their spare room. Will's folks had done the same, as had he. I wanted my bed -- my space.

When we reached the apartment I cried. My kitchen was finished. Mallie must have worked her crew around the clock to finish it. The construction mess was gone. Everything was neat and tidy and freshly painted and beautiful. I wanted to explore the whole house and see all the furniture Isabel had picked out for me finally in place. Will and Mom refused, steering me into my bedroom instead. Once I was tucked into the big bed in the master, they let BC out of the bathroom. He burst into the room in a rush, vaulting onto the bed.

"Hey there, buddy." Once I spoke he meowed, talking to me as he walked up and down me, sniffing me, inspecting me. My broken arm got a thorough inspection then he walked closer, touched my cheek with a big, furry paw, then laid beside me with a sigh.

"He is the coolest cat." Will had gotten to know him well since I'd been laid up. BC twitched the end of his tail when Will spoke but didn't move. I didn't expect him to leave my side anytime soon.

Despite my intention to stay awake, the pain meds the doctor had ordered I take made me doze off almost right away. I woke to the smell of fresh bread wafting up the stairs and an empty bedroom. I didn't remember Mom and Will leaving, so I must have passed out right away. I stretched, enjoying being in my own bed and free from the IV and all the monitors and other junk. A glance out the window told me I'd slept right through the night to the next morning. Outside my window was a crisp, blue sky scattered with fluffy clouds. It looked like a beautiful day out there. I felt restless, sick of being in bed. I pushed myself up, dislodging BC from his spot against me. He opened one eye and rolled over, getting comfortable again. I caught sight of my running shoes and wished I could put them on and go for a run. Or even a walk. I wanted to move. Staring at the cast on my left arm I sighed, reminding myself I needed to focus on making it across the apartment on my own.

I worked on that small goal the rest of the day. With BC supervising I made slow laps around the apartment. I had to take lots of breaks, pausing to lean against the kitchen islands or sit on the couch or on handy chairs. I wandered, building my strength and getting to know my renovated and decorated home. There was a collection of mismatched dishes in one of the new kitchen cabinets. In another was a collection of mismatched glasses. There was silverware in one drawer, towels in another. In the cabinets on one of the islands I found a note. *I know you'll want to pick out your own pots and pans. Call me when you're up to going shopping.* It was signed with a heart and the letter 'I' -- Isabel. She was the best. Two shopping trips with her and she'd gotten the feel for my taste and had run with it. All the things in the house were things I would have picked out myself.

Off the kitchen there was now a big farmhouse table with matching chairs. I couldn't wait to cook a meal for everyone and see them enjoying it around the table. At the front of the apartment, just past the long table, Isabel had created a little reading nook for me in a corner. Big bookcases sat between two windows, with a small table, two oversized chairs, and a tall lamp. She'd even found my small collection of books and scattered them out on the shelves. I smiled when I saw a cat bed on one of the shelves. Isabel had even made a spot for BC. Across from the reading spot, Isabel had put a big comfy couch, turned away from the windows and toward a flat screen TV mounted on the wall. She had added a low table and two more chairs making a cozy spot to relax and watch movies. I collapsed for a while

103

on the couch, flipping through the channels until I got restless again. I checked out the bedrooms next, happy to see Mom had settled in to the bedroom that shared a wall with the den. It was the larger of the two. With the transom window above the door and the new skylight in the ceiling it was a brand new room. In the Jack and Jill bathroom was another skylight, brightening up the sixties style, pink and white bathroom. It wasn't everyone's taste but I loved the quirky little bathroom. The other bedroom was transformed too. Full of sunlight thanks to the third skylight. All of my grandparents' boxes had been moved into this little room, most still closed. I was glad Mom had left them for me to go through. I felt like it was something I was supposed to do on my own.

As I worked my way around the apartment, I realized that it looked like home. Not just *a* home but *my* home. The idea scared me. That voice, that stupid voice in my head was still telling me to leave when the year was up. But it really did feel like home here. And nothing had ever felt like home to me. After everything that had happened over the last few days this had been the place I'd wanted to go. I hadn't thought about packing up my truck and blowing town. I'd thought about coming back to the apartment and the bakery. I'd thought about coming home.

At lunch Luz appeared at the top of the stairs. She took one look at me as I finished a slow lap around the apartment.

"Should you be doing that?" She glared at me, one hand on her hip, the other holding a familiar looking paper bag.

"Is that food?"

She shook her head and relented, walking past me into the kitchen. BC abandoned his post on the couch, trotting up to Luz, his feather plume of a tail straight up. He knew there would be something for him in the bag too. I followed them, passing the two big islands as I headed toward the table. I looked over my new kitchen as Luz emptied out the bag, putting a burger and fries on a plate for me and tossing BC a fry. The kitchen was just like Mallie had promised. Bright and open and better than I could have asked for. The two big islands had replaced the half wall that had once hemmed in the space. Thanks to the storage in the new islands, the pantry, which had once been a whole wall in the narrow kitchen, was long gone. Without the wall of cabinets closing in the kitchen, it was now open to the whole apartment.

The space was lighter and brighter. Like a proper home, instead of an outdated, cramped apartment. Each lap I'd walked around the apartment had reinforced my earlier realization. It was *my* home. Mine.

"You okay?" Luz's question pulled me out of my head. "Did you overdo it?"

"I'm good. Tired and hurting but good." I took a big bite of the burger, savoring my first non-hospital meal. As I ate Luz filled me in on the latest Rio Verde gossip. Two kids from the high school had been busted attempting to steal the principal's car in a prank gone wrong. A stray dog had gotten into the Walmart, leading the employees and two deputies on a wild chase before slipping out the doors and vanishing. Plans for the Halloween carnival were underway, the whole town getting excited for the event just a few weeks away. It was good to hear all the local news. I realized I was excited to hear it and excited to get back into my little place within Rio Verde society. I thought about staying put. I thought about the things I'd leave behind if I hit the road when my year was up. I thought about leaving the apartment I loved more with each slow circle around it. For the first time in my life, the idea of leaving a place made me sad.

"What's with the giant Bible?" Luz asked as she finished filling me in on the Rio Verde happenings.

I glanced over at the book when she spoke. I'd set it on the end of the table when I'd started making my laps around the apartment. I'd missed it while I'd been in the hospital so I'd been picking highlighted verses out of it at random, reading about their interpretation on my phone as I'd walked. It had made my day fly by and given me a lot to think about.

"That's the Abbott family Bible. I found it in one of the boxes a while back. I've been reading bits and pieces of it -- highlighted parts mostly. It's hard to understand, it's all in pretty formal, old English. Thankfully the internet is helping me get the meaning figured out."

"How old is old?"

Instead of answering I walked over to the book and carried it to her, sitting in the chair beside her. I opened the Bible, found the page with the printing date on it and showed her.

"Wow."

"Exactly." I showed her all the family records and the odds and ends I'd found tucked inside. As we looked through it she wondered what else might be hiding in the boxes in my spare room. Before she headed back to work she pulled out a few of the boxes for me, making me promise to call her if I found something cool.

Chapter Twenty-Three

By the time Sunday morning rolled around I could make it up and down the stairs on my own -- without having to stop for a rest halfway. I even managed to put in some work in the bakery, spending a few hours sitting on a stool icing cupcakes and cookies. I also hired another baker. Well, a temporary baker. As it turned out, Will's mom had formal training in baking and cake decorating. Not what I had expected from a woman I'd learned had once planned to be a nurse. Baking had been a hobby of sorts she'd pursued until Will and his older brother had come along. She'd offered to come work for us until someone permanent could be found. Mostly though she came to help out with Mallie's monstrous wedding cake. We'd start baking it on Wednesday to have it ready for the Saturday wedding. Four big tiers was going to be some work and I still had to perfect the flavors. Lavender was still not something I was completely comfortable with. It still surprised me to realize how close Mallie and Tres' wedding was. I paused as I headed out the door, glancing at the calendar hanging beside the laundry room door. I'd been here almost two months. October was starting today. In a week was Mallie's wedding. In three was the big Halloween carnival. Before long it would be Thanksgiving and then Christmas.

"Come on, Joy, we'll be late."

"On my way, Mom." I looked at the calendar once more. If this pace continued my required year here would be up before I knew it. As I headed down the stairs to go to church with Mom I thought about the string of Sundays that had led me here. I was happy to head to church. Maybe even a little excited. Each visit to the big church had gotten easier and easier. The music had hooked me first. I loved all different kinds of music and was a little surprised at how quickly I'd connected to the contemporary Christian worship songs. They all seemed to be full of hope -- hope for better days, hope for a relationship with God. I liked the messages they put to music. Will's father had hooked me next. Dr. Bell was a powerful speaker. His way with words got me engaged in his sermon each Sunday. I didn't always understand what he was talking about, but I always enjoyed listening to him speak.

As we drove away from the bakery I thought about my original plans to sell the place. I'd already picked out possible RVs to buy. I even had a few first destinations in mind. When I'd first made those plans I'd been excited to hit the road and see new places. I wasn't quite as excited anymore. The lack of excitement scared me. Just like my thoughts of the bakery as my home scared me. I blamed the head wound and the broken arm. They pushed all the thoughts of leaving or staying out of my head and made me focus on them alone. At least that was what I told myself.

Church turned out to be a very different experience this first post-robbery-and-beating Sunday. It was like I was suddenly a local celebrity. People I didn't even know came up, hugged me, and said they'd been praying for me. Several members of the Sheriff's Department came to see me too, assuring me they'd catch the men. After the musical part of the service I settled back to enjoy the sermon. It turned out to be all about the importance of a community. A church community. A town community.

With a jolt I realized those were just what I'd found here. I wasn't on the outside of everything for a change. I wasn't standing on the edge, one foot out the door. I was part of something and it felt nice. Better than nice. It felt good. It felt right.

*****

"Is this what it's like to be from here? To be part of some place?" I asked Will as we walked out of church as more people spoke to me, telling me they were so glad I was back at church.

108

"Yup. This is exactly what it's like. Why do you ask?" He put his hand on the small of my back, guiding me through the crowd. I started to tell him to stop but knew he'd just ignore me.

"It's different."

"Different bad?" He continued to guide me through the crowded parking lot, stepping up beside me and tucking my arm into his.

"Different..." I paused, warring with myself. The same, scared voice was telling me to run. It wasn't as loud now though. "Different good. I could get used to this."

"Is that because you've fallen madly in love with me and want to spend the rest of your life with me?" There was a laugh on the edge of his words but I knew there was part of him that was serious.

I laughed at him and stopped to wave at my mom. She was heading to lunch with his parents. They'd struck up a friendship since his mom had been working at the bakery. I knew I should have been uneasy having my mother pal around with the mother of the man I... the man who seemed to think I was going to marry him. I was happy she had friends here too.

I turned back to Will, finally answering his question. "It's because I like you and I want to spend lunch with you."

He smiled, pushing his glasses up the bridge of his nose. "I'll take it. Let's go. Picnic?" In half an hour we had two bags of food from The RWB and were headed toward what Will informed me was now our spot. The bench beside the river in the park on the edge of town. I didn't disagree with him. The fluttering butterfly in my stomach reminded me I already thought it was our spot too.

Once again we had the park to ourselves. The sunny, October afternoon had a hint of cool weather to it. The breeze had changed with the calendar and it carried a promise of a cool fall to come. I was excited for it. To see this place change with the season. To see the landscape change as people shifted into warmer clothes. Menus would start to hold more soup and chili. I loved the ending of the year. Fall and winter were magical to me. It had always felt to me that as the year ended life slowed down. I knew most people felt rushed and pressured to buy Christmas gifts and such. Being broke most of the time freed me from that pressure. I could just enjoy the changing weather and the fun decorations and be grateful I didn't have a whole list of people to buy gifts for.

"Hey," Will said, pulling me out of my head. "Where'd you just go?"

"I just realized something. For the first time in my life I have people to buy Christmas presents for. People I want to buy Christmas present for."

He looked at me like I was crazy, confusion settling over his face as he tried to figure out how I'd gotten to buying Christmas gifts.

"Don't even try to follow my train of thoughts," I said, stepping around him and settling into the sunny bench. "It's a long, winding road of crazy."

"You're not crazy." Will sat at the other end of the bench, setting the sacks of food between us and starting to unpack it all.

"I am. You should know this if you're going to keep claiming you'll marry me one day. I'm weird. Odd. Strange even. I've moved to new places by throwing darts at maps. I've lived in my Bronco more than I've lived in a proper home. I name everything." When he started to speak I stopped him. "I'm serious. The huge, stainless steel mixer in the bakery kitchen, he's Bruno. My truck is Old Faithful. I panic in new social settings but don't think twice about packing up everything I own and starting over in a new city." I ran out of steam and bit into my cheeseburger, watching Will as he ate and processed everything I'd just blurted out.

"Well, I'm way too serious," he said. "According to most people, I use words as a weapon without meaning to. If I think I know better than someone I'll run right over top of them and take charge of everything." He stopped and resumed eating, smirking at me as his words sunk in.

"I'm rarely ever serious."

"I know," he said around a mouthful of burger.

110

"I swear when I'm mad. I love bad sci-fi movies and I always talk over the previews at the movie theater."

"I love 80's pop," he said, grabbing a fry from the stack in front of me. To prove it he started to sing an old Bon Jovi song. "Whoa, we're half way there. Whoa, livin' on a prayer..." I stopped him, begging him to be kind to my ears. We both laughed for a moment before picking up our burgers and resuming eating.

I narrowed my eyes and thought for a second, determined to come up with a great confession. "Sometimes, your dad's sermons make me sleepy."

"Sometimes they make me sleepy too."

I burst out laughing at his honesty. He joined me, both of us laughing until we couldn't breathe. We might be wildly different people but I was starting wonder if maybe, just maybe...

Chapter Twenty-Four

Sunday evenings had become movie night for Mom and me when she'd moved in. We both were big movie buffs and even back when things were a wreck and we were living out of her car we always found a way to make it to a movie. When she'd moved in with me we'd started setting aside every Sunday night for mother-daughter movie time. Tonight it was Mom's choice and she'd settled on what turned out to be a favorite for both of us, the 1980's classic *Fame*.

As the movie reached its conclusion I untangled myself from the blanket I'd been wrapped up in and watched my mom as she tapped her foot along to the final song. She was like a new person. The addict who had dragged me across half the country was gone. I might be long since grown up but she was finally getting a chance to be a proper mom and she was doing a great job. She'd been my rock since the accident. I couldn't have gotten through it without her. I couldn't still be getting through it without her.

"Mom. You rock. You know, that, right?"

"What?" She turned off the TV, the closing credits vanishing and the room plunging into darkness. "Whoa. Didn't think things through there."

"Hold on." I blindly reached behind me, finding a nearby lamp and turning it on.

"Better. Now what? I rock? Why?"

"Because I couldn't have handled all this stuff without you. You've been awesome."

"Aww. Thanks, kid." She walked over and kissed me on the forehead, grabbing my empty glass, and heading toward the kitchen. I followed her, awkwardly boosting myself up onto the butcher block countertop. I ran my hand across the wood, caressing my kitchen. All the countertops in the kitchen were warm, honey-colored wood. With the lower cabinets a dusty sage green, it was like having a bit of nature in the apartment. Mallie had done so well giving me a new kitchen.

"Mom. Can I ask you something?"

"Sure, Joy-bear. Anything." She didn't look up as she washed our supper dishes. Under the glow of the light over the sink she looked so peaceful. Happy and content. It warmed my heart. I was pretty sure my question was about to ruin the moment but I had to ask.

"Who's my dad?" The three words fell out of me, landing like an anvil between us. I'd asked her only once before. I'd been ten and we'd been fighting. I'd begged to know his name so I could run away to him. She'd refused to tell me and I'd never been brave enough to ask again.

Mom composed herself, drying the dish she was holding and setting it aside. She folded the dishtowel and laid it down with gentle care. At last she stepped away from the sink and to the island across from me, boosting herself up so we were on the same level.

"First, you should know I was in love with your dad. He barely knew my name but I was head over heels for him." I started to ask a question but she held up her hand, stopping me. "He was two years ahead of me at school, popular, handsome. You know the type. He never noticed me. Not until the night we..." She trailed off, leaving the obvious unsaid, thankfully. I didn't need the details.

She took a deep breath and resumed the story. "There was a big, end of summer party down at the river. Back then it was where all the kids got together to hang out, drink, fool around. I bet it still is. Kids don't change much over the generations. He was there, home from college for a while but heading back at the end of August. Somehow, that night, I caught his eye."

Mom paused, lost in the memory. She looked out the dark window behind me, seeing, I was sure, a summer night years ago.

"We had a perfect night. We walked along the river and watched the sunset. We talked and talked about everything. When the sun was gone and the party kicked into high gear we danced and drank and laughed around the bonfire. I wasn't the best behaved kid. I'd been

113

to plenty of wild parties. I held my own with the college kids that were there. I think your dad may have been a little impressed with me. Anyway, we eventually wandered off and laid under the stars and talked and talked and..."

"You don't have to spell it all out for me. In fact, please don't."

She smiled and continued. "I thought it was the start of something. I thought I'd just found the love of my life. In the morning light I learned he'd come home from school to introduce his parents to his fiancé. They'd had a fight that day and he'd come to the party to blow off steam. He claimed to barely remember most of what I'd thought had been a magical night. It wrecked me." Her voice broke and I reached out with one bare foot, touching her on the leg, drawing her focus away from the unhappy memory. "Anyway. When I realized I was pregnant, I reached out to him. He was going to school over in Lubbock so I borrowed a friend's car and drove over one day. It didn't go well. He thought I wanted something from him. I just wanted him to know and maybe help me figure out what to do. We fought and I left. I saw him again right before you were born. He'd come home at the end of the semester to help finish up plans for his wedding in June. I ran into him right out there in the square. I was huge. We just stared at each other and I took off as fast as a nine-month pregnant girl could. I never saw him again. Not until I came back here this time."

We sat in silence. I looked away from her, trying to hide the shock on my face. I couldn't imagine being in her shoes. I don't know how she handled it all. I thought about what she'd told me and thought about things I'd seen since she'd been working in the bakery with me. I thought about the people she'd interacted with, people she'd known from her youth. Then the pieces fell into place and I knew.

"Sheriff Dodge..."

"I knew you'd noticed something."

"I just... wow. So that makes Lane my sister. I hired my sister."

"You did."

"Does he know, Mom? Know I'm his daughter? I mean he has to know, but has he acknowledged it?"

114

"He knows. I know he does. The way he reacted to the robbery... it was like a father would, not a police officer. He hasn't said the words though and I'm not going to push. Lane told me the other day her parents are divorcing. I'm not going to push anything on him while he's going through a divorce."

"Dang."

"I know. Pretty heavy stuff." She slipped off the island, walking over to hug me. "Sleep on it, Joy. Pray on it, too. You'll figure out how to handle it all. I lived it and it took me a long time. I had to forgive your father for how he acted. I had to learn to stop being ashamed of myself. People have their limits and they act stupidly a lot of the time. It takes a lot of work to accept their shortcomings and learn to care for them anyway. I got there. You can do it, too."

Chapter Twenty-Five

Monday morning I slipped out before Mom woke, letting her sleep in and leaving a note saying I'd gone to the store for groceries. I had a plan I didn't want her to talk me out of. I was detouring to the Sheriff's Department on my way to Walmart. I found it with ease, the single story Justice Center took up a whole block less than ten minutes from the bakery. It sat low to the ground, giving the impression it was squatting down, huddling close to the street. The dull tan brick and the thin, rectangular windows screamed 1970s. It looked like police departments I'd seen all over. It had to be some sort of law enforcement thing, building these serious, boring offices.

As I watched the tinted front doors people came in and out, passing by me. I was just a rock in a stream to them, still as they flowed past me. I'd thought all of Rio Verde moved at a leisurely pace. I was realizing I'd just been looking at the wrong parts of the city. Over here away from the historic homes and the quiet square, life moved at a busier speed.

I sighed and shoved my keys into my pocket then pushed my way through the doors and came right back to a stop. Instead of finding a welcoming front desk I instead found a wall and a big directory. Judging from the departments listed on the felt board before me, the Justice Center was bigger than I'd thought. There was everything from water and power offices to meeting rooms and a jail. I stared at the board, trying to find one that just said *Sheriff's Department*.

"Can I help you? Are you lost?"

I turned to see a stranger in a crisp suit staring at me. With one glance I decided he was a lawyer. I had known several over the years. Mostly underpaid ones who worked in welfare or foster care. They always looked the same though. Every single one had the same slightly frantic air about them, just like the man before me.

"Yes, I am. Is there any way you could tell me where to go to find Sheriff Dodge?"

He gave me a tacky look, almost rolling his eyes at me. It was clear he thought I was an idiot for not knowing where to find someone in this confusing building. "He's down that way," he said, pointing down a long hallway running the entire length of the building. "Last door on the right. It says Peace Enforcement Office on the door."

I looked down the hallway and turned back to thank the man who had disappeared down a short hallway nearby. I repeated my sigh and steeled myself for what was about to come before heading down the hall. The last door on the right was before me in a few short minutes. Again I braced myself and stepped through the door.

Finally I found a big welcome desk and a friendly face. The gray-haired officer smiled up at me, triggering my own smile in return. "Can I help you, miss?"

"I'd like to see Sheriff Dodge please. If he's free. Please." The big room was scattered with desks in what appeared to be a random pattern. All through it were people hurrying around. Men and women in uniform. Others in street clothes. There were even a few folks in handcuffs sitting beside desks. In my head I'd pictured it as a tiny office with a few overworked employees. It was bigger and busier than I'd expected it to be.

"I'm sure he is. Don't let all the people running around fool you. It's a quiet day for us. Who can I tell him is waiting?"

I gave him my name but stopped myself before I added *his daughter*. I was warring with my emotions. I was angry at him, but I was also nervous and a little scared. I looked up as the man hung up the phone and the sheriff appeared in the back of the big room. I watched as he walked past the desks, some of the deputies asking him questions, slowing his progress. As he got closer, I saw tiny bits of myself in his face. The constant dimple in the right cheek. The bump on the bridge of the nose. Tiny pieces of me scattered across his face. Tiny pieces of him scattered across my face.

"Hi, Joy. What can I do for you today? Have you remembered something about the robbery?" He acted the way he always acted toward me. Friendly and at ease. I felt bad. I was about to blindside him.

"I think we need to talk. Not about the robbery. About your history with my mother." I wanted to shock him. He hadn't claimed me when I'd been beaten and unconscious in the hospital. Maybe if I called him out in public he'd admit to being my father finally.

He went white when I spoke. The words hung in the air above us. The room went so silent that I worried I'd lost my volume control and had somehow shouted. I knew everyone there was listening and wondering what in the world was going on and I instantly wished I could take back my words. Dodge regained his composure fast, taking my arm and leading me toward his office. I didn't resist as he wove through the desks, ignoring all the questioning stares. I looked down and saw the gold band on his finger. He was still wearing it. Still married. He must not be public with the divorce. I was worried now Mom had misheard Lane when she'd said her parents were divorcing. I felt even more awful now. I wished I could go back and unsay what I'd said. Before I could do anything we were at his office and he gave me a look that sent me hurrying inside.

"You need to think about things before you start talking in a room full of people, Joy. There is no history between your mother and I. As far as they all know, I'm a happily married man and I don't need you coming in here and changing things."

I winced and dropped my head. "I'm sorry. I should have waited until we were somewhere private."

He sighed and rolled his shoulders, turning his head to the left until a faint pop sounded. I smiled. I did the same thing a dozen times every day.

"I know there's nothing between the two of you now," I rushed on, wanting to have my say before he could stop me. "There was once, wasn't there? On a summer night in late August. Just over thirty-one years ago."

I paused, giving him room to deny it or dance around it. Instead he sat down in the worn chair behind the desk. I took a chair on the other side in silence, waiting for him to speak.

"It was one time. One night." He looked away, his gaze landing on a framed picture on the edge of the desk. He tipped it so I could see. Beside him stood a pretty strawberry-blond woman, silver scattered through her hair. Next to her stood my baking assistant, Lane. "I was in love with Kelly. I really was. I just made a..."

He struggled to find the words so I offered one for him.

"A mistake. You made a mistake."

"Let's say I had a lapse in judgment. I was all of nineteen years old and pissed off and had been drinking. A lot."

Dodge stopped again, looking at the photo. He lifted it, gone for a second into the moment frozen in time within the frame. "That's no excuse though. I was older and I knew Susie had a crush on me. I should have been more... careful with her feelings. When she came to see me at school and told me she was pregnant. Well, it wasn't a good moment. I acted like an ass."

"She told me."

"I didn't have a happy marriage. Lane is the one good thing Kelly and I created."

"Lane said you're getting divorced."

He nodded and looked at the picture again for a second. "It has been coming for years. For over a decade honestly."

I sat silent for a moment. I wasn't sure what to say to him. The fact that he'd had an unhappy marriage felt fitting. He'd been so careless with Mom's heart. After a bit I stood, unable to stay in the same room with him any longer. I couldn't help but be angry. The smiling family in the picture got to me. Even knowing their marriage had been in shambles for years it still made me furious. Mom had become an addict. We'd lived like gypsies, never staying long enough to put down roots. I'd never known what it was like to have two parents or a loving home. I blamed him. For all of it.

"Please don't go. I'd like to talk this out with you more, Joy."

119

I held up a hand, stopping him. "It wasn't just one night for her, you know. It wasn't a crush. If you need to talk to me anymore about the robbery, call me and I'll come here. Please don't come to the bakery anymore. It's just cruel." I fled before he could say another word, angry tears filling my eyes as I found sanctuary in my truck. I sat there, forehead against the cool steering wheel, taking deep breaths until I'd regained control of my temper.

Chapter Twenty-Six

That night I hit the streets, needing to walk and clear my head. I'd kept quiet all day about my morning visit with my father. I didn't want Mom to know. I didn't want her hurt by him anymore. We'd worked all day, prebaking everything we could to free up time later in the week. We'd need all we could to get Mallie's wedding cake done. Mom had settled in upstairs on the couch with a book and I'd headed out, unable to be around her without blurting out everything racing around in my head any longer.

Normally I'd go for a run to quiet the noise in my head. Since running wasn't an option I was hoping a good walk would work. The dizziness and weakness from the blow to my head had faded fast once I'd come home. My normal energy level was back too and not being able to jog or properly bake was driving me nuts. I wondered how long I'd last under the restrictions the doctors had placed upon me. No running. No heavy lifting. I wasn't even supposed to be doing much of anything at the bakery. Restrictions had never been something I'd handled well.

I left the bakery behind in moments, turning away from the businesses around the square, heading instead toward the residential areas, hoping to find some peace along the old tree lined streets. As I walked, my brain flipped through all the jumbled thoughts like the pages of a recipe book. This was why I didn't stay in one place for long. Things got complicated so fast... so easily. I'd been here no time at all and I had a mom again and friends. A man who said he was going to marry me one day even though I was pretty certain he was nuts. I'd been robbed and beaten. I'd met my dad. Despite the mix of good and bad I was starting to call this place home.

It was terrifying and I didn't know what to do.

Eventually, my walk led me down Will's street. I stopped in front of his house, debating about walking to the front door and ringing the bell. It had been a workday for him. He was probably relaxing or eating dinner. I realized with a shock just how much I depended on Will. I'd come here because I needed someone to talk to and wanted it to be him. I was counting on him to help me make sense of it all. I didn't like depending on people and yet I was. On the girls. On my mom. And on Will. The thought rattled me just as much as the idea of Rio Verde being home.

I shook off the familiar panic staying in one place always triggered and walked up the sidewalk, ringing the doorbell before I could chicken out.

"Joy?" Surprise was all over him when he opened the door and saw me there.

"Are you free?"

"For you I'm always free. What's up?"

"Can I come in? I need someone to talk to."

He didn't hesitate. Just stepped aside and let me in. I loved his house the moment I stepped inside. Thanks to an old roommate who'd loved home improvement shows I knew it was an old Craftsman cottage. The shady front porch with the little window above was a dead giveaway. Inside it was all narrow plank wood floors and original wood details. Built in bookcases with leaded glass doors. Heavy wooden beams on the ceilings.

"Mallie did this didn't she?"

He smiled, pride shining in his eyes. "She did. Right after Tres' house. Took her no time at all. It was an easy task for her compared to his huge project."

"It's beautiful. I love it."

"Good." He led the way into the house, past a small home office where his treadmill sat by a big front window, into the living room on the back of the house. A big leather couch sat under the windows beside a fireplace covered in cream-colored stone. Opposite the couch were two matching chairs. Will took one of the chairs so I claimed the other. "Wait. Something to drink?"

I asked for some water and he dashed off, returning with two glasses. He got comfortable, settling in, completely relaxed. It was something, seeing him in his home. I was starting to realize I had just scratched the surface of this man. He had layer upon layer of interesting personality. Here in his house he was very much a guy. Not a guy in a suit. Not a guy going to work or church. Just a guy, relaxing at home at the end of the day. No suit. Not even any shoes. Just sweats and a sweatshirt. I mentally moved Post-Workout-Will down on my list. This version of him was my new favorite. This version made me want to just stay here all night, hanging out, talking.

"So what did you want to talk about?"

I tugged my cell phone from my pocket, holding it up. "I made a list."

He held out his hand and I handed the phone over. I watched as he read the list. I knew what number he was on by his face. Number three: Is operation help Luz still in progress? It drew a simple smile. Number seven: How can you be sure you love me? It made him pause and glance over at me. When our eyes met he winked then returned to the list. Number ten: Sheriff Dodge is my dad. It got a verbal reaction.

"What? Dodge is your dad?"

I nodded and sipped my water, watching him process the news. It was still strange and new to me. I was interested to get his take on it.

"Okay, well we are starting with number ten. I think I'm going to need something stronger than water." He got up and paused, looking back at me. "Is it okay? To have a beer in front of you?"

"It's okay. I never liked beer anyway." I was touched he'd asked. I'd discovered since I'd been sober, most people didn't know how to act around an alcoholic. It was like I was a bomb. Or was going to attack them for their adult beverages. In reality, I'd sort of lost the taste for it. I still missed the floaty, warm feeling I'd gotten when I drank. The feeling of not caring about anything had been nice. I was doing just fine without it though.

He came back with a bag of potato chips and a bottle of beer, reclaiming his chair.

"So, let's talk about your dad. Pretty huge news."

"Yeah. It is." I kicked off my tennis shoes and crossed my legs, settling in. I laid the whole story out for him, starting with the August night Mom had told me about and ending with my morning visit to the justice center. "I just sort of left. I didn't give him a shot to say anything. I'm just too angry at him."

"I get it. It sounds like he was a jerk to your mom but Joy, he was just a kid too. I mean, at nineteen, could you have been mature enough to handle something so huge correctly? I know I couldn't have."

"At nineteen I was on my own and had been for a year. You're forgetting you're talking to someone who's been taking care of herself like an adult since age twelve."

"Well you're a special case. My point is most people would have screwed it up just like Dodge did. Since we're being honest, your mom didn't exactly make great choices either."

I unfolded my legs, stretching them out before me. When I realized I was close enough to prop my feet up on Will's chair I did, leaning back into the chair to think a second.

"You're right. She didn't. She's only just now making great choices. My family is a train wreck."

"Yes it is. It's going to be fine though. Pray about it."

"Mom said the same thing."

"So listen to your mother."

I stuck my tongue out at him and grabbed my phone back. "How about we go back to my list?" He nodded so I pulled up my list and picked something way less personal -- my idea about helping Luz and Mateo. "We'd just started talking about project Luz's house before... everything. Did you do anything on it while I was out of commission?"

To my surprise, Will reached over and caught my hand, holding it tight. "I was a little preoccupied. Someone I care a great deal about was hurt."

"Stop it," I said, tugging my hand free as the ever-present voice in my head started to scream *run*. "I warned you, I'm not staying here. When my year is up I'm selling the bakery and moving on. I have plans. Plans that don't include staying here."

He leaned away from me, taking off his glasses, closing his eyes and rubbing the bridge of his nose. "You're wearing me out with that, Joy. Sooner or later you've got to realize you're home."

Chapter Twenty-Seven

Will and I never got through my list of things to discuss. Not very well at least. He'd updated me on the progress of the plan to help out Luz and Teo. Mallie and Tres were on board, ready to fix up the beat up little house. Things were stalled by Mateo's work schedule. Until we could get him and Luz to go out of town for a long weekend we couldn't do anything. Everything else on the list had been skipped. I quickly realized how it late it was. Since I had to be up in a few hours I tried to head home but he stopped me and demanded I let him drive me the short distance back to the bakery.

Will was still on my mind the next morning. It had been eye opening to spend time with him in his space. I couldn't help but remember things Mallie had told me about him as I worked in the bakery. She'd said he worked at the church a lot, taking charge of different groups when their normal leaders needed breaks. I could see why. He had a way about him that made people comfortable. It made you want to be around him. Perfect for a church leader. I couldn't help but wonder what would happen if his proclamation came true. If he married me -- a woman with a checkered past -- I couldn't help but worry what it would do to his future at the church. I wanted to believe the Rio Verde First Baptist Church was different from the churches of my youth, but I worried about dragging him into the world of un-Christian Christians I'd experienced.

As the day wore on it was clear I was more in the way than anything else. Will's mom Joann was a wiz in the kitchen and she and Lane worked together as if they'd been doing it for years. Mom stayed in charge of the register and everything flowed without me. I knew I'd be needed when we started on the wedding cake the next day. Today though I could slip away without being missed. So I did, escaping in my truck for a bit of alone time.

I wandered through the streets, turning left and right at random, not wanting to go anywhere but needing to move, to do, to be... somewhere. I drove through the historic district around the high school. I turned down a street, driving under the canopy of trees. Their changing leaves were starting to fall, shades of yellow and gold scattered along the red brick streets. I'd always envied the kids living in neighborhoods like this. The houses with the wide front yards and big trees. Flower gardens and front porches. Basketball hoops and driveways turned into chalkboards. All things I had never had.

I remembered Mallie saying she'd always thought living above a bakery would have been fun. I looked left, realizing I was passing her home, and paused. As my truck idled I studied the formal, serious home. It was so elegant and beautiful. I wondered what she'd think if she knew I'd dreamed of living in a house like hers.

Pressing the gas I moved on, down the street, turning right, then right again before heading down a main road toward the western edge of the city. When the Rio Verde Memorial Cemetery appeared before me I turned in without thinking. I don't know why the cemetery felt like the place I needed to be -- it just did. Winding my way through the narrow streets, I stopped when I found the fenced in area with 'Abbott' on the gate. I'd suspected my family might have something like this considering how long they'd been here. There was a certain satisfaction in finding out my guess had been right. It was odd, though, how easy I'd found it. Had almost driven directly to it in fact.

A God thing. I heard Malle's voice in my head, whispering the words. Maybe it was a God thing. Maybe I'd ended up here for a reason. Since I'd moved to Rio Verde I'd learned the Abbotts had been in the city longer than the cemetery had been here. It had been built up around the plots of the founding families - the Abbotts, the Andrews, the Coulters, and the Dodges. Four families who had picked the teacup of a valley in the Texas Panhandle as a spot for a new town. It had been a brave move at a time when most of the state's population was still in the south towards the coast. I slipped out of the truck and stood at the gate, the wrought iron chilly in my hands, thinking of

127

those first Abbotts. Mom had told me they'd come to America from England and from Italy before then. They'd come to New York first like so many others then found their way to Texas somehow. She'd told it like it was her own journey instead of the path of some unnamed ancestors. It made me wonder about this family I'd never known. About these roots I had but didn't understand.

"Joy?"

I jumped at the sudden voice in the otherwise silent day. Quickly looking around I was surprised when I saw Mallie walking down the hill toward me.

"Mallie? What are you doing out here?"

She didn't speak until she had reached me. She pointed to a tombstone silhouetted against the crisp blue sky.

"Visiting my mom. It's been just over a year."

"I'm sorry. I can't imagine."

"It's rough. Especially now," she paused, looking down at the engagement ring on her finger. "Never thought I'd be about to get married without her."

I didn't know what to say to comfort her so I was silent. She looked toward the collection of graves before me. As I watched her, it dawned on her where we were standing.

"I'm sorry. You came to visit your grandparents and I just bulldozed my way in. I'll go."

I stopped her with my hand on her arm. "Don't. I don't know why I came. I never knew them. I just went out for a drive and ended up here. I'm the one who interrupted you."

"No big deal. That's what friends are for, right? Interrupting you when you need it the most."

I paused, still not used to hearing her call us friends. I just hadn't ever been good at being a friend. It required a sort of permanence I had a lot of trouble with.

She smiled and linked her arm with mine. "Do you have lunch plans? You should come with me."

"Come with you where?"

128

"To lunch of course."

Chapter Twenty-Eight

Mallie's idea of lunch turned out to be very different than mine. I'd followed her into town, leaving the Bronco beside the bakery and joining her in her truck. Five seconds later, we pulled up to the RWB diner, Luz jogging out and climbing into the truck. I had guessed we'd go have lunch somewhere in town. Instead, Mallie headed out of the city.

"I thought we were going to grab lunch. Where are we going?"

Mallie ignored my question, just glancing across me at Luz as she drove.

"We are going to lunch. Just not to a restaurant."

The two friends exchanged another glance across me. I rolled my eyes and tried to not get angry. I felt worn thin by everything today. Being hampered by the cast and my own healing body was driving me nuts. I wasn't in the mood for inside jokes. I forced my bad mood aside though, trying to joke with them. "If this is some sort of elaborate plan to kidnap me and take control of the bakery it isn't going to work. You'll never get past Will. Or my mom. Or BC the guard cat."

They both laughed, erasing my bad mood.

"We're not kidnapping you. We're liberating you. We've been plotting to steal you away for a bit. You need a change of scenery."

I looked from one to the other, trying to figure out what they meant. "Why do I need to be liberated?"

"Because my cousin is making you follow all those stupid rules."

"Because you've worked night and day on the bakery since you got back to town."

"Because some jerks beat you up."

"Because we're your friends and it's our job to make you feel better."

I didn't know what to say. I'd thought it dozens of times since I'd come to Rio Verde but it was still true. The friendship... it was still so new and strange.

"Aww. You guys... You're just awesome."

I relaxed as Mallie drove us out into the countryside. Fall had come to the valley and away from the clutter of the city. Whole groves of trees flushed in shades of red, yellow, and orange. In town the changing trees were still scattered around. There were no big collections of color like there were out in the country. Although entire neighborhoods could have changed trees, and I wouldn't have known. I'd hardly left the city center since the accident. I had forgotten what a beautiful little valley we were nestled in. The cottonwood trees, normally clad in the sharpest, brightest green leaves, followed the river, now a golden ribbon beside the blue-gray water. All the native grasses were golden too, a pale, almost white gold. Only the farmed land hadn't changed to seasonal colors. Most of it was still irrigated and deep green as farmers tried to get in a final harvest before the cold of winter locked down their fields.

"So where are we going for this liberating lunch?"

"Mallie's soon to be house."

"Oh. Awesome. Will told me about it. Did Tres actually find it in his back field?"

Mallie didn't speak, instead slowing down and turning the truck down a dirt road. We passed a pretty farmhouse with a collection of neat and tidy barns, fat horses grazing in the pasture running alongside the road. As we left them behind Mallie told me the story of the forgotten house. How Tres had found it when he started to clear the land and reclaim the big brick barn. She told me about the big trunk she'd found under the house and the amazing truth it had held. The house about to be her home once she and Tres married had been built by the branch of her family who had helped found the town.

"It was a God thing," she stated simply. "Tres was meant to find the house. Just like I was meant to come back here and join forces with Dad to save it."

"You claim that about a lot of things." I tried not to sound skeptical but I couldn't hide it.

"Yeah, well, lots of things are God things. Your grandfather leaving you the bakery was a God thing." Luz smiled at me as Mallie spoke, nodding in agreement at her friend's claim.

"I'm pretty sure me getting beaten and robbed wasn't a God thing."

"No, definitely not," Luz said, reaching over and grabbing my hand, giving it a squeeze. "Look at the good that has come from getting the bakery though. You've got a brand new relationship with your mom."

"You met Luz and I."

"You met Will." I blushed at Luz's statement, the butterfly in my stomach turning flips at Will's name.

I was grateful when they both looked away from me, drawing my attention to the beautiful Victorian farmhouse we pulled up to. I was in awe. Mallie had done a great job redoing my kitchen but this was clearly her true calling. Saving old houses took a special touch she certainly had.

As we climbed out of the truck Tres appeared in the barn. He greeted us with a wave, shouting there was brisket in the kitchen then promised to come visit with us after awhile. He disappeared into the barn, two huskies following behind him.

"Isn't one of those your dog, Mallie?" I remembered the cream and gold dog from Sunday lunch at her house.

"Yup. Tres has his brother. When Dad and I are super busy Bugg comes out here."

"Bugg is a good influence on Trouble," Luz added, leading the way into the house. I'd expected Mallie to give me a tour but instead Luz stepped up, leading me through the first and second floor, pointing out all the original details Mallie and her dad had brought back to life. The wide plank floors and all of the trim and doors were a deep walnut brown and a beautiful contrast to the clean white walls. All the interior walls were the original shiplap and the subtle horizontal stripes made by their seams made the house feel relaxed and more homey than any Victorian home I'd ever been inside. Most were over decorated and stuffy -- too formal and fancy. Tres' house felt like a home. Like a lived in, well-loved home.

Each room reflected the history of the home -- framed deeds and photos and old farming equipment were scattered everywhere. I could see bits of what had to be Tres' personality. Mallie's too, even though she didn't call it home yet. A pair of flip flops I knew must be hers were sitting beside the couch. On the coffee table was a book on the history of farming in Texas.

When Luz ended the tour in the kitchen I found my favorite room. It was the perfect combination of old and modern. The wide plank floors continued in here, making the room tie in with the rest of the house. The cabinets were older but restored. The countertops were sleek concrete, the cool gray matching the stainless steel appliances. At the end of the kitchen, tucked into the bay window, was a small table -- old and scarred but inviting just the same. The kitchen was Mallie and Tres in every detail. Old and new.

Luz and I dove right into the big aluminum pan of brisket Mallie had pulled out of the fridge. We made simple brisket sandwiches and sat around the table, sipping tea, and sliding a single tub of potato salad around the table, each of us eating a few bites at a time. It wasn't fancy or anything but it was the best lunch I'd had in a long time.

The pair of them started a twenty questions attack as I chewed my last bite of sandwich. By then Tres had joined us, perfuming the kitchen with the sweet smell of the hay, the dust from it coating his clothes. He ate and watched them question me, amusement in his eyes. First came easy questions. How did it feel to come back to Rio Verde? How were things with my mom? How was I feeling after the robbery? Had the sheriff caught anyone yet? I fielded each one with ease, throwing questions back at them when I could. I got details on Luz's wedding and on the plans for Mallie's.

When Tres returned to work, Mallie broke out the first big question. Why did my mom run away with me? I told them the same story Mom had told me. Just like Will they were both surprised. Like so many people, they'd thought my grandfather was a gruff but kind man. The man my mother had grown up with had been very different. I couldn't help but wonder what he would have been like with me. Unbending and harsh like he had with Mom? Or the kind baker everyone else had known?

Almost like they'd planned it, they moved on fast, taking turns, asking me things they'd been dying to know. I should have been bothered by the pressure to share. Instead I was touched they wanted to know these things. Plus, the relief I felt as I shared all the things I'd been carrying on my own -- it was like nothing else. Before long the questions stopped and we were just talking, sharing things. I told them about my evening talk with Will, leaving out the plan for Luz and Mateo's house. Mallie grinned ear to ear at my admission.

"You know he's the one who found you."

"He what?" I didn't understand what she was talking about.

"He found you. When Harry died and left the bakery to you. It was Will who tracked you down. I told him to hire a private investigator but he refused. It was like working a puzzle."

"Will has never met a puzzle he couldn't solve." Luz stood as she spoke, starting to clean up the leftovers still sitting out on the counter.

"Luz is right. He's tenacious."

"I prefer pigheaded."

Mallie smiled at Luz. "Luz is still fifty/fifty on Will sometimes. He was a jerk when I came home. Now though, we're good."

"I'll agree with pigheaded," I said. "He claims he's going to marry me. Won't listen to reason at all."

"Whoa. He what?" Luz abandoned the food, coming back to the table. She and Mallie wore almost identical expressions of shock.

"Yeah. He told me the other day. I told him it isn't going to happen. I'm going to sell the bakery when the year is up. I'm going to buy an RV and hit the road. I've always wanted to just wander the country. I'm not good at standing still."

Mallie leaned back in her chair and smiled.

"What are you smiling at?"

"I think you'll stick around. I think it's a God thing."

Chapter Twenty-Nine

By the next day, I was almost convinced Mallie was right about the whole God thing. After our lunch things had sort of shifted. Two ladies from the church came by that evening with a basket of fancy bath salts, fuzzy socks, fancy lotion, several candles, and even books filled with prayers. They welcomed me back to Rio Verde and to the church family and said they were happy I was up and about after the incident. The next morning Luz's mom came by with a big tote of cleaning supplies. She announced she was going to clean the apartment for Mom and I -- said she'd felt called to come give me a hand. Mom had tried to stop her but she'd just given her a hug and sent her back into the bakery.

Neither one of us were willing to argue with someone who wanted to clean for us. We had two days to go before Mallie's wedding and the bakery had never been so busy. I'd whipped up a test version of the cake one last time the day before just to make sure I had things right. Baking with lavender was new to me and I was second and third guessing everything. I was driving Mom and Lane and Joann crazy by demanding they taste frosting and cake combinations.

"Joy, honey, the wedding is Saturday. You've got to stop changing things up. Trust your gut." I looked from Mom to Lane who nodded in agreement.

"It's good, Joy. Everyone is going to love it."

"I agree, Joy," said Joann as she took a pan of cookies out of the oven.

"You guys are sure?" They all nodded in agreement. "I just want one more opinion before I call it good."

"How about me?" I looked over my shoulder in surprise as Will came into the bakery from the side door. "I will always try something you've baked."

"Excellent. Here. Come taste." Will joined me at the work table where I'd iced slices of the test cake, each icing a bit different, trying to find the perfect combination. The lemon lavender cake was proving to be a challenge to ice. Nothing was quite the right fit with the flavors of the cake. At least, nothing was quite right to me.

"Okay. What am I tasting?"

"Nope. I'm not telling you anything. Just try each one and tell me which you like the best." I held out a fork to him which he took with a grin. The four of us watched him eat a bite from each slice, pausing to savor each mouthful, his face revealing no clues to his favorite. When he finished and sat down the fork we waited in silence.

"Well," Lane said, almost shouting at him. "Which one is your favorite?"

"They're all good." He smiled at me. "Good job there, Red."

I looked away from him, hoping I wouldn't blush. The combination of the praise and the sudden pet name set the butterfly in my stomach into cartwheels. Instead I caught both my mom and his watching me closely. I looked back to him, feeling safer with a red face than holding eye contact with the two of them.

"Thank you," I mumbled.

"You're welcome. Now, like I said they're all good but this one," he said pointing to the last in the lineup, "this one is the best. The icing is just right with the cake. Mallie's wedding cake, am I right?"

"Yes."

"Shouldn't you have nailed all this down ages ago?"

"Yes, she should have," Mom said, slipping back to the front of the shop to help a customer.

"She's right. I should have. I just want it to be perfect and couldn't quite get the icing flavor right."

"Well you did with this last one."

"Thanks. You saved my sanity and everyone else's. I've been driving them nuts." I grabbed the pad I'd left beside the cake slices, crossing out all the icing options and circling the one Will had picked.

137

A simple buttercream frosting with a hint of vanilla. A light coat of it and the cake would be perfection. Having someone from beyond the bakery world confirm the flavor combo lifted a weight off my shoulders.

"Come on, walk with me." Will headed back out of the kitchen as he spoke, backtracking through the side door. I hesitated but Lane shoved me after him.

"Go. Get out of here. You need a break and... well... we need one too." Mom and Joann both started to laugh so I grumbled and followed Will outside. I knew I'd worn them all out today, even though I wouldn't admit it out loud.

Once outside Will headed off down the sidewalk, turning away from the square. He caught my hand, tugging me along with him. We walked past several businesses, most closing up for the day. The squat line of shops soon shifted into more mixed buildings. A big, old house divided into apartments. A small church. A barber shop. I'd driven past the buildings dozens of times but I'd never walked this way. It was nice, slowing down, looking at the places I never paid attention to.

"You feel better now you're out of the kitchen?" Will asked after a few minutes.

"I do. Thanks for getting me out of there. I didn't realize how much I needed a break." I tucked my arm into his and leaned my head on his shoulder. "You're a mind reader and my favorite person today."

Will slipped his arm around my waist and kissed my forehead. For once I didn't tell him to stop it. Lately, my determination to hit the road was fading.

"I had an ulterior motive for stopping by this evening."

"Oh yeah?"

"Yeah. I wanted to know if you'd be my date to Mallie's wedding."

"I can't. I've got to get the cake there and assembled and decorated. I'll have to do everything while the wedding is going on. Then serve it during the reception."

"Nope. Your mom and Lane already said they could put the cake together and finish the decorating and a couple of ladies from the church will cut and serve the cake. They do it at most of the weddings around town. They're pros."

I stopped and stared up at him. "You arranged all of that just so I would come with you to the wedding?"

"Sure I did. I can't think of anyone I'd rather have come with me to celebrate Mallie's day. Besides. I know she'd rather you come as a guest rather than as the baker."

I didn't know what to say. Part of me wanted to be mad because he'd gone around me and rearranged all my plans. That part was silenced by the part of me touched by the gesture. By all he'd done just to get to spend the day with me.

"Well then, Mr. Bell, I guess I'll be your date. Since you went to so much trouble just for me."

Chapter Thirty

The soft jingle of the bells over the front door pulled my focus away from the wedding cake before me. I looked up, catching Mom's eye as she sat behind the register with a book. It was a quiet Friday afternoon for once. So quiet we'd sent Lane and Joann home for the day. Most of the town was busy elsewhere -- either getting ready for the Halloween carnival or getting ready for Mallie and Tres' big wedding. I was focused on other things too. Mallie's wedding cake held all of my focus today. It was hard to work with a cast on one arm but I was getting it done. Joann had stacked the tiers and put on the buttercream frosting. She'd gone on to add all of the big decorations -- stunning white flowers which added subtle, tone on tone elegance to the cake. When she'd started to add the additional simple decorations I stopped her, sending her home. She was acting as the mother of the bride tomorrow. I could finish the simple stuff. She was needed elsewhere. So I was working my way around the cake, piping on simple final details.

"It's just Will," Mom said, turning back to her book. I returned to the cake, knowing he'd come on in and make himself at home.

"Hey. Oh, cake!" Will appeared beside me, reaching out toward the cake. I slapped his hand away before he could ruin the icing. "Ouch!"

"Mallie's cake. If you ruin it I will end you."

"It looks so good though."

"You're as bad as Mallie. She was in here earlier begging for a taste." I glanced around and pointed to a stack of clean plates by the sink. "Bring me a plate and I'll make you a frosting rose."

I piped a quick and poorly made rose onto the plate he brought me, smiling as he hopped onto the counter and ate it with his fingers.

Dressed in his banker clothes with his bow tie perfectly tied and he still managed to look like a little kid as he licked icing off his fingertips.

"You know, your grandfather was right. You were born to bake."

I looked up from the cake when Will spoke. He was still perched on the counter, the plate beside him, now empty. He loosened his tie and pulled off his jacket, rolling up his shirtsleeves as he got comfortable. It did funny things to my heart to see him there. The butterfly in my stomach started to perform acrobatics, even though I looked away and refocused on the cake.

"Like I said, this is my world."

"I get it." He tapped on the wall behind him. "Over there is my world." I knew he didn't mean the hardware store.

"Really? The bank?" I set down the piping bag, flexing the fingers in both hands. Decorating a cake with a broken arm was a new challenge for me. I was realizing just how much you need both hands to handle this sort of work. "Mallie told me you used to be the youth pastor at the church. Why'd you step back from that role?"

He looked down, twisting his bowtie through his fingers. It was the only time I'd seen him look sad -- no, heartbroken. I wanted to rush over and hug him or something. I stayed where I was though, picking up the piping bag again and going back to work. Will stayed silent for a while, gathering himself.

"It wasn't the right place for me," he said at last. I waited, certain there was more to the story. "I wanted it to be. I wanted to follow in Dad's footsteps. Jackson has. He's like Dad, a gifted preacher. I'm good with kids. Dad gave me a shot. I screwed it up though. I'm just glad the bank could use me full time and I had someplace to go."

I sat the bag down and crossed the short distance to him. I didn't say a word, just took the plate, walked back to the center island, created another big frosting rose, then walked back and handed it to him. Just like I had hoped, it made him smile.

"You're not a screw up, Will. Trust me, I know. My family helped found this town. Look at how badly Mom and I have screwed up. Over and over. You will never take the Biggest Disappointment crown from the Abbott girls, my friend. We'll hold the title for at least a few generations."

"She's right. There's screwing up and then there's us." Mom chimed in as she joined us in the kitchen. "I'm going to run, kiddo. I still need to find shoes to wear to the wedding."

She got her purse from the office and walked back through the kitchen pausing before Will. She laid her hand on his arm.

"Just remember, Will. Your folks are proud of you even if you don't follow in your father's footsteps. I'd be proud of this one even if she decided she wanted to become a circus performer or a politician. Do what makes you happy. That's all a parent ever wants."

Mom stopped again at the register, looking back at us. Her gaze settled on my cast clad arm. "Are you sure you can finish the cake with your arm?"

"I can, Mom. It'll just take a while."

"Okay. Will, stay here until she's done and help her get it into the freezer."

"Yes, ma'am."

Will and I both watched her leave, staying silent until her car drove past the bakery.

"I like your mom," Will said with a smile.

"She's growing on me, too."

"She's not who she used to be, is she?"

"Nope. She's changed herself. I wish she could have done it sooner, but I'm happy she's done it." I stepped away from Will, going back to the cake once again. "Now. What'd you screw up?"

"It doesn't matter. It happened and I've stepped back. I like the bank. I like helping folks learn to manage their money."

"It matters. Tell me but first hand me the pastry bag over there." He looked to where I was pointing and brought me the bag. Almost all of the cake was snowy white, crisp and clean. All of Joann's big details had been white. The details I'd been adding had been bright white too. The bag Will had just handed me was full of the palest lavender icing I'd been able to create. Mallie hadn't wanted it to be a flowery, super feminine cake. Tres hadn't wanted a groom's cake so it was his cake too. All the decorations had been simple and elegant, nothing showy. Now I would add a single outline of faint purple to each layer. Nothing more. Not even a bride and groom topper.

"The cake is beautiful," Will said, reclaiming his spot on the counter.

"Thank you. It's not my taste, but it suits both Mallie and Tres well."

"What would you do for your wedding cake?"

I looked over my shoulder at him and then glanced down to the neon pink tank top I was wearing. "I like bright colors. I've always thought a cake covered in rainbow sprinkles would be fun. Like packed into the frosting. Every inch of it."

Will chuckled as he picked up his plate, scooping up a big pile of frosting with two fingers. "I like it. It would be cool. Very you. We'll have to do it."

I rolled my eyes at him, shaking my head then bent back to the cake. "We have never even been on a date. You kissed me one time. We're not getting married."

"Tomorrow's our first date."

"I know."

"I'm kind of excited to take out the pretty redheaded baker."

I couldn't help it. I smiled. He called me pretty and the butterfly went crazy and I grinned at him like a fool. I couldn't have stopped myself if I'd tried.

"You can't avoid telling me what happened by flirting with me."

"Sure I can," he said, catching my hand and kissing it.

"Oh quit. Go in the office and look at the books. Let me finish."

He kissed my cheek and disappeared into the office. I heard the computer power up and returned to the cake. I piped the fine line of purple around and around, finishing off each tier of the cake with the subtle hint of color. When I was done, the leftover icing went into the fridge. I'd use it to frost cookies or something in a few days. I turned back to look over the cake. It was simple and yet elegant. Perfect for Mallie and Tres.

"Will, can you help me get the cake into the freezer?"

He reluctantly stepped away from his spreadsheets and rejoined me in the kitchen, helping me carry the huge cake to the big walk-in freezer. I'd already put a card table in there for it. Tomorrow, Mom and Lane would put it in a big box and take it the few blocks to the First Baptist Church in the back of my Bronco. The church had a big meeting space where the reception would be held. It was on the other side of the church from the sanctuary so they would be able to set up the cake well in advance and keep it away from Mallie and Tres. It gave them a chance to just be guests instead of skipping the wedding to set the cake up at some secondary location.

"All done," I said, shutting the freezer. Will headed back to the office, but I stopped him. "Hold on. Take a second." I turned away from him, pulling open the big door to the loading dock, sitting down on a little bench beside it. Will joined me with a heavy sigh. For a while it was silence between us. From our seat we could see cars driving by and between the buildings, a slice of sky slowly turning from blue to sunset gold.

"It was one kid," he said. "One kid I somehow missed. Somehow didn't see the signs."

I didn't speak, just took his hand, lacing my fingers with his, waiting for him to keep going.

"Lexi Tyler. A quiet girl. I missed it. I didn't see her withdrawing from things. I didn't see her getting sad and curling into herself. She tried to kill herself. Last August. Thank God, her brother found her and called 911. She's better now. On medication, learning how to live with depression. I should have seen it. I should have been someone she felt safe turning to for help. So I stepped back. Then the leadership team found new youth leaders. Mike and Katy are so much

144

better at it than I was. Those kids liked me, but they love them. It was the right thing to do. I wanted it to be my thing, my gift. It isn't though."

I leaned my head on his shoulder, trying to offer him comfort with my contact. He leaned into me, squeezing my hand.

"It's okay, you know, if it isn't your gift. I think helping people like you've helped me is your gift. You've taught me lots of stuff. You've made me better at taking care of this place. I'm betting you're helping lots of people every day. You may not see it, but I bet you do."

"Thanks, Joy. I needed to hear that." He kissed my forehead, making me close my eyes and smile. "Now, back to work. I need to balance your books and you need to close up shop."

Chapter Thirty-One

"Mom. Are you sure this looks okay?" I stood in the doorway of her bedroom, clad in the vintage dress she'd found in one of the boxes stored in the other bedroom. It was straight out of the late 60s. Cocktail length, high necked, and sleeveless. The yellow-green silk fell away from the neckline in relaxed pleats making it both fancy and super comfortable. Luz would be over here tomorrow once she saw it. When she'd helped me pull out a few boxes the other day she'd made me promise to share any vintage clothes with her. I'd already set aside several outfits I knew she'd love.

"Wow. Joy-bear you look amazing."

"I still can't believe this was my grandmother's dress." I walked over to the mirrored closet door and looked at my reflection. I'd piled my wild hair up in an attempted messy updo. Mom had tweaked it a bit and made it work. The color of the dress played off my red hair and fair skin making me look very Irish. I wondered if we had any roots leading to Ireland. The one thing throwing off the outfit was the cast on my arm. I glared at it and looked away. It wasn't going to come off in the next five minutes so I had to make due.

"I don't ever remember seeing her wear it, but it was in the box of her stuff. I'm betting she wore this right around the time she and Dad married. Maybe on their honeymoon, or to their engagement party."

She appeared in the mirror behind me and smiled at me. I took in her outfit with a quick glance. Jeans and a long sleeved tee shirt. Just put a cake together clothes. She'd refused to get ready until Will and I left. On the bed, her outfit was waiting. She'd opted for vintage too. In the same box holding my dress she'd found a 1970s era jumpsuit. It had looked like it was made for her when she'd tried it on. All black with a halter top and a wide, shiny leather belt. Perfect for her. I knew what Mallie would say when I told her about finding the clothes. *A God thing.* Out of all the things saved this box of clothes had held things both Mom and I had loved. It was too perfect to be a coincidence.

The doorbell for the side door sounded, making us both jump. I dashed out of the room, racing to put on my shoes. Simple taupe suede pumps I'd picked up years ago at a vintage shop in Seattle. I slipped them on and stood at the top of the stairs, knowing I was missing something but drawing a total blank.

"Your shawl." She tossed the balled up crocheted shawl to me. I caught it and shook it out. The color of pale sand and soft as BC's fur, the shawl was another of my vintage finds. I wrapped it around my bare shoulders, happy for the warmth. The October day had turned cool, a front dropping down on us that morning, bringing thin gray clouds and a hint of rain. I said a quick prayer, hoping it would stay away until after the wedding.

"Purse," I asked, scanning the apartment as Mom dashed away to search. I immediately saw I'd hung the multi-colored clutch on the doorknob by its wrist strap. "Found it!" The doorbell rang again as Mom appeared in the doorway of her room.

"Go. I'm right behind you."

I clattered down the stairs, sending BC darting into the bakery kitchen as I rushed to the door, flinging it open and making Will jump in surprise.

"Sorry, sorry. I lost my purse for a second. Let's go."

"Woah. Stop." He caught my arm as I rushed passed him, turned me to face him. "You look beautiful."

While he looked me over I took him in too. He'd gone for a navy and navy look -- navy slacks and a sharp navy jacket with a clean white shirt and dark brown casual shoes.

"No bow tie."

"Nope."

"Hmm."

"What?"

I headed to his waiting car, making him follow me.

"What?"

I stopped, looking at him over the top of the car. "I like your bow ties. They're kinda hot."

"Red, you keep saying stuff like that and I'm going to have to kiss you again."

I winked at him and slipped into the car with a smile.

*****

"Can I draw on your cast?" I looked over at the little boy who'd appeared beside me, holding a marker in one hand as he eyed the blank slate of my pristine cast. I'd been watching Mallie dance with Will, the two of them laughing hysterically as they circled the dance floor. Mallie was breathtaking in her dress -- all cream lace and beige satin. A vintage Art Deco dress that could have been created just for her. Her honey blond hair was in loose waves that just kissed her shoulders. She'd opted for no jewelry and was in simple ballet flats. She was beautiful. Deliriously happy and beautiful.

"Please?" the boy asked again and I made myself focus on him.

"Why do you want to draw on my cast?"

"Because it needs a monster on it."

"A monster?"

"Yes, ma'am."

I studied him for a minute, fighting a smile as I tried to stay as serious as he was. "Who are you?"

"I'm Taylor."

"Taylor who? Do I know you?" My second question made him giggle.

"I'm Taylor Bell."

"Is your uncle that guy over there?" I pointed to Will, still trying to stay serious. This kid in his little suit with a pair of wire frame glasses on his face was a tiny Will. It was all I could do keep from scooping him up and loving on him.

148

"Yes, ma'am." Will caught us looking and smiled and waved.

"Is the monster going to be scary?"

"Yes, ma'am." He paused, going all thoughtful. "Not too scary, though."

"Okay then. Go for it." I set my left arm on the table and he hopped up in a chair, sitting up on his knees and leaning over my arm. He studied the cast for a moment then started to draw. It took just a second or two for his father to spot what he was doing and hurry over. Jackson had been a surprise when I'd met him at the wedding earlier. I'd expected the same sort of seriousness Will always carried with him. Jackson though was always on the edge of a laugh. He was infectious and drew people to him like a magnet. I understood now what Will had meant when he'd said Jackson was born to the ministry. He had something special about him -- something a church leader needed.

"Oh no, now Taylor, what are you doing to Miss Abbott's cast?"

"He's drawing me a monster. I'm certain it will be amazing. Right, kid?"

"Yes, ma'am," he said, smiling at me and then his dad. Jackson and his wife Gia were written all over their little girl, six year old Sophia. She had her mom's out of control curly caramel hair and her dad's warm brown eyes. Taylor though, at a very mature eight, was just like his Uncle Will. They were both precious kids. I was enjoying watching them run and play. I was especially enjoying watching Will with them. He was excellent with kids.

"You're sure about letting him do that?" Jackson asked as he pulled up a chair.

"Oh yeah, it's fine. The beauty of being the quirky baker is no one will bat an eye if I have a big monster on my cast. They've kind of gotten used to strange from me."

"Well, good then cause I can't vouch for his artistic ability. He takes after his mother, you see, and she can't draw to save her life."

Taylor giggled as he worked. I smiled and glanced over at Gia. Will had told me she was a pretty accomplished artist. She'd painted

149

murals in all the Sunday school classrooms at their church and had her art hanging in several galleries in Oklahoma. I watched Taylor work, not surprised to see a pretty good monster taking form on my cast.

"Dad, I need another color." He sat up and held out his hand to his father. To my surprise Jackson reached into his suit coat, pulling out a handful of markers.

"Which one?"

"Red."

Jackson held out the red marker, taking the black one Taylor had been using.

"Taylor, what are you doing? Jackson, why are you letting your kid draw on my girl?"

"First a pet name. Then I'm your girl? Pretty sure of yourself there, Money Guy."

"Yes, I am. And yes, you are. You just don't know it yet." Will kissed me on the forehead and swatted Taylor on the butt with a laugh. Just when I thought I'd seen all the sides of this man I saw him with kids. With kids, especially his nephew and niece, he was a new person. Laughing, joking, saying the right things to draw them out and make them feel special. I decided Will around kids was my new favorite version of him. He claimed the chair beside his brother but not before reaching across the table and taking the piece of cake sitting in front of me. I glared at him and he just grinned and winked, eating my cake without a bit of remorse.

"Dad. I need green now."

Jackson traded markers again with Taylor then turned to his little brother. "What's up with you, brother? Calling Joy your girl? Something you need to tell me."

I watched Will close, wondering what he was going to say to his brother.

"I'm going to marry her one of these days."

"What?" Jackson shot a glance at me and I caught him looking for a ring on my hand. Taylor distracted him, demanding a blue marker this time.

"No, he's not. This is our first date. We're not getting married."

"Sure we are, Red."

I rolled my eyes at him and looked back at Taylor as he worked away. I tuned out Will and Jackson, just watching the boy draw. He traded markers with his dad a few more times then sat up with a smile on his face.

"All done!"

"Okay. Let me see this masterpiece." I held up my arm, turning it so I could see the whole monster. Taylor's artwork took up about half the cast and it was wonderful. A big blue monster, red clawed hands held out to the side, his wide mouth with green teeth open in a snarl, the black eyes glaring away. It was a masterpiece.

"Taylor, this is the best monster I have ever seen. Thanks, buddy." Taylor hopped out of his chair and raced away, most likely looking for something else to draw on. Jackson followed him as he dashed off, a loving-but-tired-Dad smile on his face.

"Let me see this monster," Will said, sitting down in the chair Taylor had vacated.

"Your nephew is pretty good."

Will studied the drawing then looked across the room to where Taylor was now playing with a group of kids. Pride glowed all over his face.

"He's a great kid. I can't wait to see what he grows up to be."

"I'm sure he'll do amazing things."

"He will." He leaned back in the chair, focusing all his attention on me. "You having a good time?"

"I am. It was a beautiful wedding, and it's been a fun party."

"I'm sensing a but."

I started to speak but a yawn escaped instead, making Will chuckle. "I'm exhausted. What time is it?"

"Maybe eight thirty, Grandma."

"I know. I'm used to baker's hours. Even though the shop was closed today I still was up by five this morning. My body is programed for early mornings and early bedtimes."

151

"So let's go." He stood, holding out his hand.

"No. I'll go. You stay with your family."

"No. I'll see them tomorrow. Now I'll take you home."

I started to argue but another yawn took control so I stood, taking his hand. We made our goodbyes, getting hugs from everyone. Mallie's hug lasted the longest as she whispered, voice full of tears, how much the cake had meant to her. *My mom would have loved it. It was like you found a way to make it seem like she was here.* By the time we broke apart both of us were weepy. I promised her we'd have a girls' night out when she and Tres got back from their honeymoon.

When we finally escaped into the quiet evening I was yawning almost nonstop. Even the crisp, cool air didn't wake me up. I dozed off the minute I sat down in Will's car waking with a start when he gently shook my shoulders. Before he had even reached the other side of the square I was upstairs climbing into bed. It wasn't until morning I noticed he'd added something to the artwork on my cast.

Will Loves Joy was written in his neat handwriting on the underside of the cast right in my palm where no one but me would notice it.

Chapter Thirty-Two

Thanks to all the extra members of the Bell family I was able to avoid Will in church the next morning. Between the love note on my cast and his second surprise I'd found while I was eating breakfast, I was nervous about talking to him. I'd pulled up my to-do list on my phone, planning to check things off and add a few more only to find he'd gotten there first. Number one on the list now read "Marry Will." I was half amused and half angry. I was also one hundred percent sure I didn't know how to handle it. How to handle him. He caught my eye several times during church, the expression on his face a mix of humor and question. I knew he was trying to see if I'd discovered his question and if I'd made a decision. I knew he'd want to talk and would probably even invite Mom and me over for lunch. So I yawned a lot and pretended to be exhausted. Mom caught on to my plan and backed me up, telling everyone we were headed home to go through all the boxes left in the apartment and take naps. No one questioned us and we were able to escape everyone with ease.

"So, you want to tell me why I just lied to the preacher's family?" Mom waited until we were in her car before she asked. I was thankful for her restraint.

I answered by holding up my phone, showing her the addition to my list. Her eyes went wide when she read it.

"Will?"

"Yeah."

"What are you going to do?"

I looked out the window, watching the town pass by the window, trying to think of how to answer her. "I have no idea, Mom. I'm not sure how I feel about him. I'm not sure I even want to get married. I'd never even thought about it. Hell, I still don't even know if

I'm going to stay here when the year is up. I don't know anything. I'm just..."

"Overwhelmed?"

"Very."

With a complaining squeal, she stopped her car beside the bakery, turning it off and looking over at me. "Come on. I have something that might help you sort things out in your head." She was inside the bakery before I could unlock my seatbelt and get the door open. I cursed the cast for once again frustrating me. I still had six weeks left in the darn thing and was pretty sure I wasn't going to make it. I was already wondering if I could con Mallie into sawing it off for me when she got home from her honeymoon.

"So?" I asked when I reached the apartment.

"So what?"

"What do you have for me?"

Mom shooed me toward my bedroom. "Go get comfortable first. I'll make you a sandwich for lunch."

"Do I not get to stay here?"

"No. You need to go somewhere away from people and TVs and work and even purring cats. Some place where you can be free from distractions."

As I changed into jeans and a sweater, I thought of places that would fit Mom's description. I ran through places I thought would be empty on a Sunday afternoon, soon landing on the one place I knew no-one would bother me. The bakery roof. I'd slipped up there a few times since the robbery, watching the sun rise and set over the city. It was private, the hardware store had no roof access and the bank past it had another story on us and no windows looked down on the roof. It also felt safe. There was just the one way up and down -- a set of pull-down stairs in the utility room. Mom had even helped me get some lawn chairs and a little table up there. I pulled on a jacket and grabbed a spare blanket from my bed as I left the room. When I walked into the kitchen Mom held out a little sack lunch for me.

154

"Lunch and this." She held out a book wrapped in a bright blue silk scarf. I unwrapped it, surprised to see a worn Bible with a green leather cover. *Nancy Louise Durand* was embossed in neat, gold script on the lower right corner of the cover.

"It was your grandmother's. She got it when she was baptized. I found it in one of the boxes of books the other day when I was hunting for something new to read. I'd noticed you were reading the big Bible. This one might be a bit more portable and easier to understand."

"I'm not sure..."

"Just trust me, Joy," Mom said, cutting me off. "When nothing else could help me, when I was at the bottom, the word of the Lord was the one thing... the only thing that helped. Give it a chance, kid."

"Okay. I'll try anything. Now, can you pull down the stairs for me?"

She smiled. "I thought you might want to go up there. They're already down." She hugged me then handed me my lunch and the Bible. Before I could walk away she caught me and tucked a bottle of water in my jacket pocket. "Take all the time you need. I'll be right down here when you're ready to talk."

I thanked her and climbed up to the roof, leaving the rest of the world behind me. I settled into one of the chairs and ate my lunch. Then I sat there, the Bible in my lap, my hands laid over it, watching the city. I was high enough for most of the city sounds to become muted, indistinct white noise. Since I'd drug the chair over near the bank wall I was also hidden from anyone nearby. The solitude was exactly what I needed. As I sat there, watching clouds dance across the sky, I felt all the noise in my head settle and start to fade.

Opening the Bible, I turned the pages at random, just like I'd been doing with the family Bible. I didn't know the scripture well enough to know what to look for or even what questions to ask but I was starting to trust in a higher power and knew somehow I'd find the right words.

"A God thing," I whispered as I flipped the pages. Mallie's expression. It had become mine too, even though I admitted it only to

155

myself. Those God things she'd talked about were becoming very real to me. More and more often little moments were adding up to bigger things. I stopped turning the pages and looked down, scanning the text until an underlined verse jumped out at me.

"Don't worry about anything; instead, pray about everything; tell God your needs, and don't forget to thank him for his answers." I read the words in a hush, just loud enough for my own ears. A God thing again. I was a worrier. Always had been. I guessed my grandmother must have been one too for her to have underlined this verse. I set the Bible aside, face down, still open to those important words. I wasn't sure how to pray about all the things running around in my head. The worry about what could go wrong if I dared to stay put. The fear about risking my heart with Will. All those things and more weighed on me day after day. Finally I closed my eyes, lifting my face toward Heaven, and began to pour it all out to God.

Chapter Thirty-Three

I sat on the bakery roof for most of Sunday, praying, reading my grandmother's Bible, and trying to figure out what to do. My whole life felt like it was stalled, sitting at a fork in the road. I had to make some decisions. I couldn't stay stuck forever. By the time I climbed down the stairs to the apartment the day had turned gray and cold, the promise of rain carried on the wind. Mom appeared at the bottom of the stairs, holding out a hand to take my blanket.

"Feel better?" she asked as she folded the stairs back up into the ceiling.

"I don't know. Maybe."

"You want to talk?"

"Not right now. I would like some dinner though. I'm starved." We decided on pizza and called what had become our favorite place -- a little restaurant just a few blocks away that could get pizza to our place in less than fifteen minutes. In no time at all we were sitting down to dinner, BC appearing from one of his hiding spots and taking up residence on the kitchen table, begging for bites of sausage. We ate in silence and cleaned up in silence. Both of us retreated to our bathrooms without a word. It had become our normal routine. We spent most days in a state of constant motion. Constant noise. Talking to each other. Talking to customers. Evenings were for quiet. As soon as Mom had moved in I realized how much alike we were. Even though we both enjoyed working with people all day, by the end of the day we were ready to be quiet and withdraw into ourselves a bit. It was our recharge. Mom would read. I'd often go back downstairs to work on the books in my pjs. She protested, worried about me working downstairs alone. I wasn't going to let what happened make me afraid in my own place.

Tonight, however, was different. I'd brushed my teeth and changed into pajamas and thought about crawling into bed. I knew I needed to talk things through though and I knew Mom was the right person to talk to. So tonight I changed our routine.

"Mom. Can I ask you something?" Mom looked up at me from the little reading corner at the front of the apartment. She was curled up in one of the overstuffed chairs, book in hand. I'd sat in the same spot many nights since I'd gotten out of the hospital. We both gravitated to the corner. Reading, thinking, and sometimes just watching the world go by. We both wanted to sit there most evenings. The similarity, the connection to someone else, the reflection of me in her and her in me, was something I didn't know I'd wanted until I'd found it.

"Always, Joy-bear."

I joined her in the little corner, claiming the other chair in the pool of light cast by the tall lamp behind her. I didn't speak right away, instead looking around the apartment, taking in how different it looked now. The wrecked kitchen was gone and replaced by a beautiful, open kitchen. The loss of the walls that had once closed it in made the apartment look huge. It was a brand new place. It felt like a home.

I turned back to Mom and found her watching me.

"It looks pretty different, doesn't it," she said as she tucked a bookmark between the pages of her book and set it aside. She shifted in her chair and looked back at the apartment. "Dad would probably hate it, but he was always impossible to please."

"It's a home now. It felt like a trap when I got here but now..."

"You've made it yours and that changes a place. You've put your stamp on it."

"Exactly." I slipped back into silence, again looking over the apartment. Mom was right. There were pieces of me all over the place. Pieces of her too, I noticed. In the time since she'd moved in she'd made it her home too. It wasn't Harry and Nancy's place anymore. It was Susie and Joy's place. *Also home to BC the wonder cat.* He appeared in the kitchen, jumping onto the countertop and into the kitchen sink. He loved to lounge in there.

"So, what did you want to ask me?"

I turned my focus back on her, tucking my feet under me as I got comfortable in the chair.

"How did it feel? Falling in love with my dad? How did you know it was love and not something else?" I felt like a child asking her those questions. At my age I should have understood those things but I didn't. I'd never been in love. I had never let myself get invested enough in someone to allow feelings to go so deeply. I'd never connected with someone in such a deeply personal and frightening way. Love had always fascinated me. Not in an I-can't-wait-to-fall-in-love sort of a way. More in a distant way. I always felt apart from love. Like an outside observer studying a foreign culture.

"Why do you want to know?"

"Because someone is making me wonder."

"Would someone be a dark skinned banker with a fondness for bow ties?"

I felt my cheeks warm and looked away for a moment. "Maybe."

"I thought so. He is a very good man." She laid her hands over the book in her lap and studied me for a few moments. "Why are you unsure about your feelings for him?"

"I just... It's confusing. I've never let myself feel like this about someone before. I always take off before I can form these sorts of connections with someone. It scares me. Staying put, making myself a home. Making friends. Trusting someone enough to let them near my heart. It has always felt like a trap to me."

"When he drops by the bakery, are you happy to see him?"
"Yes."
"Do you think about him when he's not around?"
"Yeah, a lot."
"What does it feel like when you do see him?"

"There's this butterfly in my stomach. It goes nuts when he's around."

"Do you find yourself wanting to touch him or be close to him?"

"Yes. He's like a damn magnet."

She smiled softly, knowingly. "Sounds like you're falling for him, darling. I felt the same way about your father back in the day."

"Well crap. I didn't want to fall for him. I planned to sell this place and move on after a year. I did. I made all these plans for after the year was up."

She laughed, a quiet chuckle and smiled again. "That's pretty much how it works, Joy. Your heart does the falling, not your brain. Like Mallie would tell you, it's a God thing. Maybe all this happened so you and Will would find each other."

"It's those damn bowties and the wireframe glasses."

"They do make him look very handsome."

"I never thought I'd fall for a nerdy guy."

"Smart is sexy."

"It so is."

We both laughed at my admission. I didn't know what to do with these feelings. I didn't know what came next. I'd always split before I could reach this point with anyone.

"What am I going to do, Mom?"

"I think you're just going to have to love him, kiddo. I think you're going to have to give in and let yourself fall."

*****

The next day Will came by the bakery after he got off work at the bank. We weren't open but like always I'd left the front door unlocked for him. He'd get on me for leaving it unlocked -- the guys who'd broken in were still out there after all -- but I didn't care. I was dizzy and lightheaded the instant I saw him. Naming the feelings I had for him had made the butterfly in my stomach multiply. Now there was a whole swarm of them dancing around in excitement. I didn't know what to say to him. Or if I should say anything. I did know I wanted him to kiss me again. Thirty-one years old and I just now understood the whole fuss about falling in love.

I tried to be cool. I watched him wander in, pausing to visit with Mom who was sweeping the floor, getting ready to open tomorrow. He was wearing his banker clothes -- navy suit with a striped dress shirt and a bowtie in shades of gray. The damn bowtie just about did me in.

"I'm in love with a nerd," I whispered to myself. I forced my eyes away from him and back to the loaf pans I was washing. One handed washing required a level of concentration I'd lost the moment he walked in. When I reached into the soapy water to drain the sink I snuck one more glance at him through the open doorway. Then I promptly knocked the stack of clean pans into the sink, soaking myself with the dirty water. I couldn't help it -- I let out a quick scream of shock, making both him and Mom turn to stare.

"You okay?" Mom started toward me but I waved her off.

"I'm fine. I just splashed myself. I'm going to go put on a dry shirt. Will, make yourself at home. I'll be right back."

I reached back into the water, this time pulling the drain plug without further soaking myself, then headed toward the side door, hoping to make a quick escape. Instead I ran right into Will.

"Oh wow." His struggle to stay composed was visible and he quickly lost the battle. A laugh rumbled out of him. "Maybe the hot pink bra wasn't the best choice today." I glanced down and gasped when I realized what he'd meant. My once invisible neon pink bra was now visible thanks to the wet tee shirt.

"Oh my gosh." I quickly folded my arms across my chest, feeling my face flush. "If you'd just excuse me I'm going to go try and salvage some of my dignity." He stopped me as I tried to slip past him, catching my hand and halting my progress.

"Wait. Your mom said you had something to tell me."

"What? No, I don't." My cheeks burned and I knew I'd gone as red as my hair. I looked past him as Mom peeked around the corner, smiled, then disappeared. "Okay, yeah I do but we're not having this conversation when I'm wearing a transparent tee shirt. Come on up."

Will released me and followed me up the stairs. I ducked into the master bedroom, tossing aside my sopping wet shirt and reached into my closet, putting on the first thing I grabbed.

"I'm not sure you made an improvement there," Will said, a laugh ending his sentence.

I glanced down and flushed again. Of course. I'd put on a shirt that said *Cake Dealer*.

"I swear. This isn't my day. Just pretend it isn't a dorky baker shirt."

"I'm not sure I can. That is pretty nerdy."

I stood there staring at him, thinking again about how much that bowtie of his got to me. Without a word I crossed the space between us, catching his face between my hands, standing on my toes and kissing him. I put everything into the kiss. Everything I couldn't bring myself to say, leaving both of us breathless.

"Is this what you wanted to tell me?" he asked, catching me and pulling me close again for a second kiss. The butterflies in my stomach were going into orbit. It was wonderful and amazing and I hoped he would always make me feel this way.

"Pretty much, yes."

"I may need you to repeat it. Just to be sure." He grinned at me, mischief dancing in his brown eyes.

I stood on my toes again, touching his face more gently this time. "I can do that," I said, touching his lips with mine.

Chapter Thirty-Four

"Y'all, I am worn out." I looked out over the city as Mallie spoke, too tired myself to agree. It was Thursday evening in the middle of a busy week. The inky black of evening had come fast, settling over the city like a thick blanket. Cars drove by, people walking past, shopping or having dinner. It was a busy night on the square. No one looked up and saw us perched on the roof of the bakery. Mallie and Luz sat on either side of me, each of us with our feet propped up on the edge, comfortably sitting in the row of folding chairs, blankets over our laps. Mallie had been back from her honeymoon for a week and this was the first night we'd all been free to get together. A fourth chair sat empty, waiting for Isabel to join us.

"Me too." It was Luz who spoke. I looked over at her and smiled.

"Me three. This week has been exhausting."

In some way, each of us had been part of the chaos of the week. We'd all been roped into helping with the city's Halloween carnival. Mallie had been building booths and other things. Luz and I had been making all sorts of food. Isabel had been painting Mallie's booths. The carnival was tomorrow. I didn't know about my friends but I was about equal parts excited and ready for it to be over.

"Hey, y'all. I'm sorry I'm late." Isabel appeared behind us, climbing through the opening, a pool of light around her. I wasn't surprised when I saw BC appear on the ladder next. The cat had to be in the middle of everything. Isabel claimed her spot, remarking on what a great place to hang out it was, then handed Mallie the brown paper bag she'd been carrying.

"What's this?"

"A bit of carnival food, in advance."

Mallie opened the bag, whooping with joy when she saw what was inside. "Churros... and they're still warm." She passed them out and we slipped back into silence, each of us enjoying the cinnamon sugar treats. Mallie, Luz, and Isabel sipped on glasses of red wine while I popped open a can of Dr Pepper. I caught a whiff of their wine and all I could smell was the alcohol. It smelled like rubbing alcohol to me now. Nearly three years of sobriety was finally killing the appeal of adult beverages.

"Did y'all hear there was another robbery?" Mallie made the announcement over a mouthful of churro. Part of me hoped I'd misheard her but my gut said I hadn't.

I looked down at my cast, bright white in the darkness as it peeked out from under the sleeve of my jacket. "Where now?"

Mallie explained the story she'd heard. A feed store way out in the country had been hit. The employees and two customers had been locked in a back room. The robbers had taken all the money and cellphones from everyone, cleaned out the register and the safe, and then driven off in one of the customer's pickups. No one had been hurt this time. The rumors were already spinning, claiming it was the same gang of thieves who had been robbing businesses all over the panhandle this year.

"Has the sheriff said anything to you about them, Joy?" Mallie paused, reaching for the bag of cookies I'd brought for our girls' night. "Oh my gosh, what are these?"

"Gimme," Luz said, holding out her hand. Mallie passed the bag to her, taking two more cookies before sharing. I snagged one for myself as the bag hovered in front of me for a second.

"They're triple chocolate. No, Dodge hasn't said a word to me about it."

"Then why is his cruiser over here so often?"

Luz was right. He was at the bakery a lot. My request that he stay away hadn't been respected. He still stopped by often. Now I avoided him as much as possible, just like Mom did. If Lane had noticed, she hadn't said a thing. She seemed to just always be happy to see her dad.

"Shouldn't you be working over at the diner instead of watching what happens over here?"

"I'm a very good multi tasker," Luz said over a mouthful of cookie.

I realized I hadn't told them my big revelation. I'd told Will and talked about it with Mom, but I hadn't looped them in. I took a sip of my drink and decided now was as good a time as any to do some sharing.

"Well, for one, you guys forget his daughter works for me now. For two, because he's my dad and is trying to make peace with Mom and I."

"Shut the front door!" Luz dropped the bag of cookies as she spoke. I smiled at her, then glanced over at Mallie and laughed. Her mouth was wide open, shock all over her face. I leaned over and saw an identical expression on Isabel's face too.

"Yup."

"The sheriff knocked up your mom." Mallie clapped a hand over her mouth, surprised by her own words.

"Yup," I said, laughing a bit at her.

"*Dios mio*," said Luz, her hand over her heart.

"You sound like Mom when you say that," Isabel pointed out.

Luz dropped her hand and glared at her sister.

"So are he and your mom together?"

"No. They don't even talk. Mom won't talk to him. He's still married."

"He's getting a divorce."

"How do you know?"

"Working in a diner has some perks."

"Luz is right, he's getting divorced. Mom still loves him, I think. She told me he was the love of her life. I find it hard to believe. Who meets the love of their life at sixteen?"

"My parents did," Luz said, sipping her wine.

"I knew Tres was the one from the time I was a kid."

"Really?"

"Yup," they said in unison.

We fell silent, each looking out over the lights of the city as we sipped our drinks and ate our junk food. I wondered if Sheriff Dodge still loved my mom. Had she been the love of his life? Had they been meant for each other only to get derailed by his foolish actions and eventual marriage? I glanced down at the statement written on the palm of my cast. It was almost invisible in the darkness but I still turned it down, away from my friends. It had felt good to tell them about my dad but I wasn't ready to talk about Will and me with anyone other than Will. Or my mom. Or with the Lord.

Chapter Thirty-Five

"Mallie, hold up a second. I want to show you something... um... Mom and I found in my grandfather's stuff." It was a terrible lie. If Luz and Isabel hadn't been so tired they would have called me out. Instead they just waved goodbye as they shuffled down the stairs.

"You're a terrible liar," Mallie said with a laugh as the sound of the door closing bounced up the stairs.

"She always has been." Mom appeared in the doorway of her bedroom, clearly having just been woken up.

"Sorry, Mom. Go back to bed."

She waved us off and joined us in the kitchen, pulled a box of chocolate mint candies out of the freezer. She set the box on the counter, opening it and unwrapping one of the mints.

"Midnight snack."

"So," Mallie said, pausing to grab a candy. "I'm guessing you want an update on The Big Plan."

"Please. I feel like I haven't been doing my share."

"You got the ball rolling and gave me a beautiful wedding cake. You've done plenty. Beside, Tres has done most of the work." She boosted herself up on the counter and laid out his plan for Mom and me. Once Tres had realized his little sister was living in a falling apart house he'd gone to work. He had loved my idea to give the place a facelift as a surprise and had come up with a genius plan. He'd convinced one of Mateo's coworkers to come to work one day with raffle tickets to sell for his kid. The grand prize was a four-day trip to a bed and breakfast in San Antonio. What Mateo didn't know was there was just one ticket. Monday when Mateo got to work he'd find out he'd won the fictitious raffle.

"That's amazing. Tres is brilliant."

"It's why I married him," Mallie said with a big grin. She'd been grinning the same way since her wedding day. One side benefit of moving around a lot and making friends easy was that I'd been invited to a lot of weddings over the years. Either as a guest or as the cake maker. I'd seen a lot of brides and a lot of newlyweds. I'd never seen one happier than Mallie.

"So next weekend then?"

"Yup. Half the town is in on it. We've got just enough time to get it knocked out before my knee surgery. It's going to be great."

I glanced down at her knee when she mentioned the coming surgery. I'd stopped seeing the big black brace over her jeans. I knew though the damage done to her knee in the accident that had ended her ballet career was painful. This surgery was supposed to be one of the last shots at being able to have a functional knee again.

"Are you nervous?"

"About the project? Not at all. Dad and I have got this."

"No, goof, about your surgery. A total knee replacement -- pretty huge."

Her face fell a moment then she gathered herself back up. "I am a little. Tres and Dad already moved a bed to the first floor of Tres' -- our -- house. So no stairs to worry about but I won't be able to work. Or drive."

"We'll help out," Mom said, covering Mallie's hand with her own. It was a very mom-type thing to do and made me smile.

"We will," I added, catching Mallie's other hand with mine.

"Aww. Y'all. You're just awesome." She hugged us both then said her goodbyes, ready to head home for the day.

Mom put away the candy and turned off the lights in the kitchen as I slipped downstairs to lock up the side door. When I returned to the apartment she was back in the doorway of her room, waiting in the pool of light for me to come back up. I locked the door to the first floor and then the one to the fire escape. I had started the ritual after the robbery. Even though I didn't have nightmares or anything, I slept better knowing we were locked up safe each night.

"It's a good thing you're doing, for your new friends," Mom said, stopping my path toward my own room. "Helping Luz and Mateo. Offering to help out Mallie. Even working on stuff for the carnival. It's a good thing. You're making a home here. It makes me happy to see you settling in to this life."

I looked at her, her words sinking in. *Was I doing those things? Settling in? Making a home?* For a split second the old panic bubbled up. It whispered to me to run away before something bad could happen. Then I looked up and saw my mom's sleepy but happy face and the panic was gone.

"It is a good thing, isn't it?"

She nodded and yawned and slipped into her room. I stayed there, watching until the bar of light under the door vanished and I knew she was settled in. Then I tipped my face toward Heaven and whispered a quick prayer of thanks. Making a home -- it wasn't as scary as I had always thought it would be and I had the Big Guy in Heaven to thank for it all.

*****

Halloween carnival day started at sunrise the next morning. Before Mom and I were all the way awake and functional voices started echoing up to us from the square. Luz had warned us it was going to be an all-day thing but I don't think either of us was prepared for that reality.

"There are already booths opening up. It's seven in the morning." Mom was peaking around the corner of one of the front windows, still in her pajamas, mug of coffee clutched in her hands.

"I'm so glad we decided to close the shop today. I don't think we would have gotten any proper business. Just people hanging out in there." I was hiding in the kitchen, far from the front windows. I was still sleepy from my evening with the girls and the busy week. I wasn't ready to deal with Carnival Day. I wasn't even really ready to deal with breakfast. I'd jumped out of my skin a few minutes earlier when my toast shot out of the toaster. It had woken me out of a half asleep daze giving Mom a good laugh. I yawned, grabbing my plate of toast and an apple, heading for my bathroom. I was going to take advantage of a day off from the bakery and have a long hot bath and a slow start to my day for once.

"They just fired up the first of the barbecue grills," Mom shouted to me from across the apartment. I smiled. Mom was apparently going to people watch and give me a play-by-play of the start of the carnival.

The sun was at a more acceptable height in the sky by the time I re-emerged, much more prepared for the day. Mom had abandoned her post by the window and was instead getting ready herself. I fed a complaining BC and headed down to the bakery. My fridges were full of baked goods for the booth Mom and I had decided to sponsor. It was being run by the local branch of a nearby university and all the proceeds were going to support an addiction counseling program in the area. We'd jumped at the chance to support the kind of program that had saved both of us from our addictions. I unlocked the front door then headed back to the kitchen to start staking up the boxes of cookies and muffins.

When the front bells chimed, I smiled. Without looking up I knew it was Will. Since our magic moment a few days before I just knew on a sensory level when he was close. I wondered if it was the same for him and made a mental note to ask him.

"Hi. Are those all for me?" He grabbed at one of the boxes and I swatted his hand away.

"No. The ones for you are in the little blue box over there."

"Aww, Red, you really set aside some for me?" He hugged me and kissed me on the forehead and reached for the box, smiling when he saw it was a box of the pizza sourdough rolls. Since the evening I'd made them for him they'd become his favorite meal.

"In case you don't want to eat carnival food all day."

170

This earned me a proper kiss, which Mom interrupted way too soon. She cleared her throat making us both jump away from each other like guilty kids.

"Are you here to help us carry all this stuff, Will? Or to maul my daughter?"

"Mom." I rolled my eyes at her, grabbing a box, balancing it on one hand. Years of waiting tables in my teens had given my excellent balancing skills, something I had become very grateful for ever since the cast had claimed my left arm.

"I was hoping to do both, to be honest, Ms. Abbott."

"Susie," she corrected.

"Susie," he added, watching me with a big grin on his face.

My face warmed and I headed toward the front door before either of them could see. If this is what having a family felt like, I wasn't mad.

Chapter Thirty-Six

"Joy, walk with me."

The demand came from Tres. I hadn't seen him all day. Although, I'd been tied to the booth since late morning so I hadn't seen any of my friends. I'd just seen cookies leaving with customers. I watched my new friend carefully as I handed a customer their bag of cookies. Broad shouldered and looking like a farmer crossed with a cowboy crossed with something else. Same old Tres. Yet something was different in him. His wedding ring flashed in the sunset light. A simple gold band but it had changed him. Not in a bad way. There was a quiet happiness about him now. It suited him.

"Mom?"

"Go. We're almost out anyway. Lane and I can close up shop." I chanced a quick glance at Lane. She was her usual self. She had been happily helping us all day. It was obvious Dodge hadn't told her the big secret yet. In the back of my head was a worry that, when he did tell her, I'd lose a great employee. More than anything I was worried I'd lose my chance at a sister-type relationship with her. I'd been trying to build a good friendship with her so she'd see me as more than just a boss. I didn't want her to vanish from my life when Dodge finally came clean to her. I pushed my worries away and I joined Tres on the sidewalk in front of the booth.

"I'm all yours, Tres. Where to?"

"Nowhere. Let's just walk around."

We started to wander through the carnival and I enjoyed getting to take it all in. The whole square had been transformed. All along the sidewalks were more booths, each with food or games. In the street across from The RWB a big tent had been put up to hold a haunted house. There was a small maze of stacked hay bales for the little kids on the street to the south of the square and a stage for a band in the north street. People were starting to migrate toward the stage, anticipating the music and dancing part of the carnival. I hadn't known what to expect but I was overwhelmed by it all. It was fantastic. The whole town plus most of the nearby towns had shown up. As we walked, I spotted Isabel and the youngest of the Martinez kids, Marisol, working in a face painting booth. Tres' parents were manning another of the food booths and waved as we walked past. I knew Mallie and her dad were around somewhere along with Luz, Mateo, and little Maria Isabel.

"I wanted to thank you, Joy, for noticing what I hadn't noticed. My sister needed help and I was so busy farming and getting ready for the wedding I missed it."

"Sometimes you need an outsider to spot stuff for you. It's no big deal."

He stopped walking and looked over at me, his pale blue eyes serious.

"You don't get it, do you? You're far from an outsider. You're one of us. You have touched the lives of so many people. People you don't even realize you've affected."

The praise made me feel like a spotlight was shining on me so I looked away from him and resumed walking around the square. Tres wasn't deterred though and caught up to me in two strides.

"I'm serious. Did Mallie tell you what you've inspired us to do?"

I glanced over, wondering why she hadn't told me. "No. What?"

"We're going to see about becoming foster parents. We were talking on our honeymoon about kids, and Mallie told me that ever since she'd met you she had started thinking about fostering and adopting. I didn't know you grew up in the foster system. It bothers her, thinking about other kids, living within the system until they eventually age out like you did."

I didn't know what to say. I stopped walking and stared at Tres, overwhelmed. He smiled and, to my surprise, pulled me into a big bear hug, lifting me off the ground.

173

"You've changed our lives, little baker," he declared as he sat me down.

"Oh my gosh, stop. You're embarrassing me." I felt my face warm and pushed him away with a smile. "Let's talk about the plan. Everything ready to go?"

We looped around the square a second time, talking out all the details for the Luz and Mateo project. All the building supplies were stashed in two of their neighbors' garages. There were people on tap to show up with horse trailers and moving vans to load up all their stuff and store it for the four days we'd be working. We had crews set up for the electrical work and plumbing. Even a city inspector had agreed to help with quick permits and inspections so we could do the work without getting a big fine. Everything was ready to go. As the band started to warm up we ran into Luz and Mateo. I couldn't wait to see their faces when they came home to a renovated house.

Chapter Thirty-Seven

"Oh wow."

"I know."

"Can we fix this in four days?"

"Damn right we can." Mallie smiled over at me then turned to the rest of the group. "Okay, y'all. First things first. Let's move all the furniture out. Leave the bedrooms for now. Let's get the main rooms cleared out first so work can start there right away."

She was like a general leading her troops into battle. When I started to follow Tres and Will into Luz and Mateo's crowded living room she stopped me, her arm lowering before me like a gate.

"Nope. You're not lifting anything big, missy." She looked at my cast-clad arm.

"Looks like you should be taking it easy too, bossy pants." I nodded to the big brace she wore over her jeans, the metal and neoprene caging in the damaged joint.

"She's got a point, *mija*." Tres weighed in as he and Will walked past us carrying the big couch. It had dominated the room but didn't look so massive being carried out past us. Will nodded, agreeing as he followed Tres with his end of the couch.

Mallie's dad agreed next, walking between us carrying a big coffee table. We stepped aside, giving way to the line of people carrying furniture out the front door to one of the trailers waiting beside the house.

"I'll get the light things. Like pillows."

"Okay and I'll step back and focus on a plan of attack."

Before long all the furniture from the den and the kitchen had been packed into the moving van waiting outside. It would go park somewhere nearby but out of the way soon. Two big stock trailers were waiting for all of the furniture in the bedrooms. Mallie was putting people on project after project, moving at a quick pace. I was learning fast to trust in her determination. As the day wore on, she took the lead on everything, putting most of the crew to work on pulling out the old, stained carpet running throughout the house. Her dad and I took on the task of cleaning out the two bedrooms, pulling Tres in to help when we needed to carry mattresses and big furniture out of the house. As soon as those last two rooms were empty they were freed from the nasty carpet too.

After the carpet was out of the whole house it became a divide and conquer type of project. Mallie and I sat on the floor, tugging out any carpet staples left behind. Tres and a big part of the crew climbed on the roof, repairing everything they could before darkness shut down their work. Will and Mr. Andrews started on the smaller repairs inside fixing sticking doors, crooked cabinet doors, and painted shut windows.

We stopped working when Marisol showed up with dinner for all of us. A round of fresh workers was showing up as I left. I watched as Mallie turned the reins over to one of her employees. He'd move forward with sanding the floors and pulling out the broken and stained kitchen countertop, plus whatever else Mallie could think of for him. In the morning the floors would get their first coat of stain and work on the outside of the house would start. Mallie had a massive list but there was a massive crew so I knew it would get done.

*****

"You did a good thing here, Joy Claire." I looked up when Will appeared on the dark porch beside me. He groaned as he sat down beside me.

"You okay there, old man?"

"I'm all of six months older than you, so shut it."

"Oh, you did not just tell me to shut it."

He smiled, taking off his glasses, rubbing his eyes as he spoke. "No I did not. Clearly you're exhausted and hearing things."

176

"Ah yeah, must be." I yawned and leaned my head on his shoulder. "So I did good."

"Yeah you did, Red." He captured my hand, giving it a squeeze then leaning his head against mine. "I'm proud of you."

I didn't answer, instead letting the evening noises fill the silence. Luz's neighborhood was full of young families. In the three days we'd spent working here I'd enjoyed watching everyone come and go. Kids playing outside, families going for walks. It had been like getting dropped in a movie set. Or it had been for me at least. I'd spent most of my life searching for the things I saw around me along this little street.

I'm not sure when I had decided to stay in Rio Verde. Maybe it was when I first got here. Maybe it was when I woke up in the hospital and found all my new friends watching over me. Maybe it was when I realized my mom wasn't going to take off again. It didn't matter though.

"Y'all, I'm beat." Mallie wandered out of the house, sitting on the edge of the porch beside me. She lay back on the dusty floor and closed her eyes. "One more day though and we're done."

"Excellent." Tres joined us on the porch, claiming the last bit of space beside Mallie. "Joy, thank you for thinking of this. I feel stupid for not thinking of it myself."

I started to protest, saying it wasn't a big deal but Mallie and Will stopped me, both echoing what Tres had said. I went silent, just letting the moment wash over me. I had worked hard all day with my friends to help two more friends. It was a first for me. I'd never made these sorts of friendships. I'd never let anyone get this close but with these people I'd never had a chance to back away or put up a wall. They surrounded me with unquestioning friendship from almost the first second I'd hit the city limits. I had no idea how I'd gotten so lucky.

"You guys, I think I'm gonna stay here. After my grandfather's year is up." I paused, not looking at any of them, instead staring out into the dark street. "I think I'm home."

"Good." Mallie broke the silence, sitting up and giving me a one armed hug. "I'm pretty sure my cousin wasn't going to let you leave anyway."

"You got that right," Will said, giving me a quick kiss then slipping his arm around my waist. I leaned into him, soaking it all in. I wasn't sure what the future was going to hold. I still wasn't sure if he was the one. I was sure I was home and I knew I was going to stick it out and see what happened. That was enough.

Chapter Thirty-Eight

Luz was crying. No, Luz was sobbing. Happy sobbing. Mateo, always stoic and silent was crying too. They clung to each other in the middle of their renovated home. All around them, standing in doorways and even looking in the windows, were all the people who had worked non-stop over the last four days to complete this miracle.

"Y'all," Luz squeaked at last. She took a deep, shaking breath, pulling herself together. "Y'all did all this? In four days?"

"Half the town pitched in. Mallie had crews working non-stop." Tres stood in the kitchen, arm slung over his wife's shoulder. "Everyone loves y'all and wanted to do something to help out the two of you for once."

For once. I hadn't understood what Luz and Mateo meant to this town until I'd worked side by side with so many of the residents. As we'd worked, person after person had told me stories about Luz and Mateo. Luz, who would take meals to anyone she knew was ill. Mateo, who fixed cars for nothing more than the cost of the parts for anyone too broke to afford a mechanic. Luz, who had been a candy striper at the hospital as a teen and still went up there in her free time to help out where she could. Mateo, who did odd jobs for all his neighbors, always refusing any pay. They were part of why this town was an amazing bubble of kind, caring people with old fashioned values and kindness. I'd always been somewhat humbled by their easy and almost instant friendship. Now, though, I was humbled by their selflessness and goodwill. I thanked God I got to call them friend.

"It was a God thing," Mallie said, reaching over to tug me into view. "Joy came up with the idea. If she hadn't ended up here, none of us would have ever known how much the two of you needed help with this house."

Luz crossed the room and pulled me into a teary hug. Mateo wrapped his arms around both of us. The strength of their hug took my breath away.

"Okay, you guys, you gotta stop before I pass out," I whispered. For a second they both just hugged tighter then let me go with a laugh. The rest of the evening person after person walked through the house, praising Mallie for her vision, all of the crew for their hard work, and me for coming up with the idea. It was another one of those moments that made me love this town. These people. Everything.

*****

Things shifted again in my world the following Sunday. Dr. Bell, Will's dad, cornered me after the early service. I followed him away from the milling groups of people -- half heading home, half heading to Sunday school. I wanted to follow the crowds, to go anywhere other than down the quiet hallway to his office. I followed him though, reminding myself that he wasn't anything like the old school preachers in bad movies. I wasn't going to get a lecture on my wicked ways from Dr. Bell. Not that I had any wicked ways anymore to get lectured about.

"Please come in, I just want a few moments of your time. I'm sure you've got plans for your Sunday that don't include hanging around here." He smiled as he gestured to the pair of chairs before his big desk. I couldn't help but notice how similar it was to the desk in Mr. Coulter's law office. I wondered if the lawyer and the preacher shopped at the same furniture store.

"Oh just errands and laundry. Both can wait. What would you like to visit about, Doctor Bell?"

"Please, call me Noah," he said, settling into the big leather chair behind the desk. "My son came to me the other night and told me you're having a bit of a struggle dealing with something. Specifically someone. He didn't name names but he did tell me you recently found out who your father is and were struggling with his identity and the related emotions."

"I don't know what to say. I didn't expect him to tell anyone about our conversation." I wasn't mad. I felt like I should be, but I wasn't. Instead I was touched that he cared enough about my problems to seek advice from his father.

"Don't think of it as someone telling their preacher. Think of it as a son reaching out to his father."

"I'm not sure if that helps." I sat even though I didn't want to stay.

"My son cares about you a great deal, Miss Abbot."

"Joy," I corrected.

"Joy," he repeated, smiling. It was Will's smile. I'd never noticed it before, how similar the two of them were. It made me like him a bit more. Made him less intimidating. "As I was saying, Will cares about you a great deal. More than I've ever seen him care about a young woman. So I wanted to reach out to you. I know you grew up without a father. Maybe I could help you deal with the struggle of getting to know your father now, as an adult."

He paused, watching me. I wasn't sure what to say. So I just watched him back. As I studied him, I noticed again how much Will favored him. It was like getting to see what Will would look like one day. The only thing missing was those little wire frame glasses and one of Will's bow ties.

"Sheriff Dodge is my father." I blurted it out, shocking both of us. I hadn't planned to say anything. I'd been thinking of thanking him and making a quick exit. My mouth, on the other hand, had other plans. "He's my father and he wrecked my mom when he dismissed her when she told him she was pregnant. He has made no claim on me. Not told his wife and daughter about me. Even though his daughter, my half sister, is now working at the bakery with Mom and me."

"Well, that was not what I was expecting. No wonder you're struggling with it all."

His kindness and openness was all it took. All the tangled thoughts that had been churning in my brain since Mom had told me came spilling out. I told him the story Mom had told me. I told him about confronting Dodge at the Justice Center. I told him all about my conflicting emotions. The anger at my father for what he did to Mom. The happiness at finding out who my father was. The frustration with a reality so different than the fiction I'd created in my head as a kid. Every bit of it just flooded out of me. When I was done he offered me prayers and someone to talk to anytime. He advised me to not act on my information but to pray until I had everything sorted in my head.

"While I've got you here, I'd like you to know I'm sorry for the way your mother was treated when she was carrying you."

"You weren't even here then." I was surprised by the apology. Dr. Bell hadn't taken over the church until almost a decade after Mom and I were gone.

"I know, but I'm still sorry. The behavior she faced came from an attitude I spent a decade working to correct. I hope you'll find those old thoughts and behaviors have changed. No one wants a teenager to become a mother. As a church, though, they should have showed her support and understanding. They should have offered to help her instead of making her feel ashamed. She should never have been made to feel as though running away with you was her only choice."

His words overwhelmed me. I'd said them all to myself several times over. To hear them from a church leader, from a person I really respected... They healed something inside of me -- the something that had been hurt on behalf of my mom for years.

"Thank you. For both the talk and the apology. And for the advice. I needed all of it. Probably more than I realized." As he stood and reached out to shake my hand we heard the music start to play, signaling the start of the second service. "Sounds like you've got to go back to work."

Glancing at his watch, he agreed. As we parted ways out in the hall I thought about the events of the last few weeks. I'd never had a problem with God. It was people who had always let me down, who had always made me distrust them. It looked as though God was working to show me people weren't so bad. It seemed like another one of Mallie's God things was at work in my life.

Chapter Thirty-Nine

For once I had the bakery to myself. Sunday was always a quiet day, but normally Mom was around. Today though she'd headed to Lubbock with Will's mom for a day of shopping and fun. I'd camped out at one of the bakery tables, right beside one of the sunny front windows. Stacks of paper were spread all over the table I'd chosen. On the floor was a box of binders I'd picked up at the store. In the window, basking in the sun was my ever-faithful feline assistant. Organizing my own recipes and the ones left behind by my grandparents was a gargantuan project. Perfect for a cool November day and much better than sitting in front of the computer in the office going over the books.

I smiled as the sounds of Ella Fitzgerald filled the bakery. Soon Louis Armstrong joined in, the song making me sway back and forth as I sorted recipes. One of Mallie's last projects upstairs had been to move the only piece of furniture my grandfather had specified be kept in the family -- a big Victrola stereo record player -- down to the bakery. Well, it had been her crew's last job. The record player was monstrous. It had taken us a while to find a spot for it, but we ended up tucking it into a corner at the end of the display cases. To our complete surprise, it had still worked when we'd turned it on. Mom had even found two boxes of records in among all the boxes of my grandparents' stuff. So now we had Ella and Louis and more to sing to us all day. The customers loved it. A few had even brought us records, adding to the collection of 1930s and 1940s jazz and blues.

I frowned when a shadow appeared across my table. Looking up, my frown deepened when I saw Sheriff Dodge on the other side of the glass. He was out of uniform in just jeans and a worn jacket of chocolate brown leather. He looked tired. His hazel eyes had faint dark circles under them and it even looked as though there was some more gray in his salt and pepper hair. I locked eyes with him and he smiled a worn, half smile and pointed to the door. I sighed and thought about shaking my head no and sending him packing. Then I remembered my conversation that morning with Dr. Bell. *Give him a chance, Joy.* So I nodded and rose, walking over to the door and unlocking it.

"Joy," he said walking inside. I expected him to go right to the table and claim one of the empty chairs. Instead he looked around the bakery a moment, restlessly walking a zigzag through the scattered tables and chairs.

The record player slipped into silence so I ignored Dodge and put a new album on the play. Frank Sinatra filled the bakery, soothing me with his velvet voice. I reclaimed my chair and gestured to an empty chair, finally getting him to settle and sit.

"What can I do for you, Sheriff?"

"You don't have to call me Dad, but how about you at least call me Walter."

"Does this mean you're admitting to being my father?"

"I am. I came to see you today to tell you I've told my wife -- my now ex-wife. I've told Lane, too. I'm not sure you'll be seeing her at work on Tuesday."

"No big deal. She can take all the time she needs. Or even quit. I'd hate to lose her, but I'll support any choice she makes."

"That's a very big sister kind of thing to say."

I didn't answer him, instead picking up a stack of paper and squaring up the pages. I set it aside and reached for another one, tidying up my mess a bit. "I'd like to be a big sister to her. A friend, too. I have missed making way too many memories with her. I'd like the chance to make up for it."

"You're not the only one who would like to make up for a missed lifetime."

I looked up from my papers, surprised to see tears in his eyes. For a man who had spent his whole adult life carrying a gun and chasing bad guys, the emotion came easy to him. He was more than

I'd thought he was. Kinder. More caring. He reached over and took my hand.

"I'm sorry, Joy. I'm sorry for how I treated your mother. I'm sorry I never gave her a chance. I think... I *know* we had something more between us than just one night. There was a spark there I feel like I should have paid attention to. Susie... your mother will always be my 'what if' girl. What if we'd met sooner? What if I hadn't been engaged? What if, what if, what if. I will always regret those unanswered questions. Just like I regret not being a father to you when you were younger. I know it is probably too little too late, but I'd like a chance to be in your life. To be some sort of a parent to you even though you're already an accomplished woman."

I stared at him, weighing his words. If he'd walked up and said them to me four months ago I would have just turned around and walked away from him. A lot had changed since I'd come to Rio Verde. Those four months had reshaped a lot of things in my world and a lot of things in me. I never thought so much could change in so short a time. Or that it could all be good, happy changes. With all of those thoughts in my head I smiled, softening toward him.

"Okay," I said. "Let's give it a shot, Walter. Tell me about you so I can get to know my father."

We talked for around an hour that afternoon. I learned about what growing up in Rio Verde had been like for him. It was wildly different from the life my mom had described. While she'd had super strict parents and a suffocating life of rules and restrictions, Walter had run wild and free across the whole county. He'd been his parents' golden child and had gotten to do anything he wanted. Free from curfews and such, he had been able to just sort of float through life. By the time he looked at his watch and declared he needed to go, I had learned a lot about him. I still wasn't sure how the wild, carefree kid had ended up becoming a cop but I did at least know him a little.

As I watched him walk back down the sidewalk and disappear, I thought about how strange the day had been. Cornered by the preacher. Cornered by my father. All I wanted to do was have a quiet afternoon sorting recipes. Instead I had a mind full of heavy life type stuff. I sat for a while longer, trying to get back to my project. My mind refused to focus though so I gave up. Locking the front door and scooping up BC, I headed upstairs and to the Bible Mom had given me. I knew it was the exact thing I needed to help settle my mind and give me the clarity I was looking for.

Chapter Forty

"Would you have dinner with me tonight?"

"Joy?" Will looked up from his computer, surprised. He'd been so engrossed in his work he hadn't heard me. With his secretary gone to lunch, I had been able to slip in unannounced.

"Yes. Will you? Are you free?"

"For you, I'm always free. Where would you like to go?"

"Your house. I'll cook for you."

"You can cook?"

I couldn't help but smile at the question. People always asked me that. As if baking and cooking were so different that one couldn't be good at both.

"Trust me, I can cook. Can I have your keys? I'll have dinner ready for you when you get off work." He started to say something and I just held out my hand and gave him a look, daring him to make a smart remark.

"Okay. Here you go. There isn't much in the fridge."

"Don't worry. I'm going shopping. See you tonight." I turned to go and he called out to me. When I turned back he came out from behind the desk, caught me by the hand and pulled me close, kissing me.

"You just made my Monday, Red. See you tonight."

*****

"Do I smell steak?" Will's sudden voice made me jump. He appeared in the doorway of the kitchen, looking tired but happy.

"Yes, you do smell steak. Told you I could cook." I smiled as he shed his jacket and pulled off his tie, setting both over a chair, relaxing in an instant. He joined me in the kitchen, boosting himself up

188

on the counter and grabbing a tortilla chip from the big bowl I had sitting nearby. He sat there munching on chips and salsa and told me about his day. Working in a bank sounded boring to me, but the way he talked about it told me it was work he loved. He told me about all the people he worked with and all the inside jokes and drama.

"Mrs. Irby came in today. You haven't met her yet. She's a hoot. Eighty some odd years old. Doesn't drive, so she walks all over town. As she walks she picks up spare change and once a month comes in and deposits all the change. She always makes the teller count it out in front of her by hand. The tellers will hide when she comes in. It's always fun watching them try to scramble over each other, each one trying to take their break first."

When I started to get out plates, Will jumped off the counter and took them from me, setting the table as I set out the food. It was the first meal we'd eaten on our own. It felt familiar though, like we'd been having dinner at the end of the workday together for ages. He fixed both our drinks as I put our steaks on plates, adding them to the table then returning for the last part of the meal -- a cheesy potato casserole I'd found in my grandmother's recipes. I'd found it the other day, right before my father had derailed my recipe-organizing project. I had been trying to organize everything a little bit each day but I kept getting side tracked by things I wanted to cook. With each recipe, though, my grandparents became less and less of a pair of strangers to me. As I understood what they liked to cook, and bake, I developed a stronger and stronger picture of them.

I pulled my focus back to dinner as Will and I sat down, facing each other across the table. Will surprised me when he reached out his hand, waiting for me to place my hand in his. When I did, he lowered his head and started to pray, blessing our meal and thanking the Lord for bringing me to Rio Verde. I was speechless, only able to whisper amen when he'd finished.

Will dove into his steak, eating so fast I started to wonder if he'd eaten all day. Given how busy he usually was, it was possible. I ate with more leisure, trying to understand why he'd thanked God I was back in town.

"So, let's talk about your day. What'd you do with your day off?" He'd paused in his assault on the food, smiling at me. "Excellent food, by the way. You're a genius in the kitchen."

"Why'd you thank God for me coming to town?"

He stopped eating and stared at me, studying me. I wanted to look away or distract him but instead held his gaze, waiting for him to answer me.

"Because I'm thankful He did. More than thankful to tell you the truth." He paused, eating another bite, then started to speak again. "Did you know my mom's folks disowned her when she married my dad? Just because he's black. Mom always says he just has a much better tan than her. Then she points out how fair she is and says everyone has a better tan than her, so it isn't a big deal."

I chuckled, resuming eating. I could tell he wasn't done yet even though he ate a bit more before continuing.

"Anyway, when Mom's folks found out she was marrying a black man they lost it. They would have kicked her out of the house but she was already on her own. They didn't come to the wedding. They halfway kicked Mallie's mom out of the family because she did go. Stood beside her sister because to her it didn't matter. Her sister was happy and it was all she needed to know."

"I can't imagine how hard that was for her. Especially given how she'd been raised." When he'd first told me the white side of his family had been white sheet wearing racists, I'd been surprised. When I'd gotten to know his mom I'd been even more shocked. She was the most colorblind person I'd ever met. I imagined her sister had been, too, because Mallie was the same way. I couldn't wrap my head around how the two women had become that way when they'd been raised to hate anyone with darker skin than their own.

Will stopped to eat again, closing his eyes and smiling as he ate some of the potato casserole. He whispered "so good" as he ate a few more bites before resuming the story.

190

"It was a little girl at school that saved Mom and Aunt Tess. She was Aunt Tess' friend. She invited Mom and Tess to church. Mallie's named after her."

"Really? Their parents didn't stop them from going to church and learning not to hate?"

"You know, I've never asked Mom. That's not my point though. My point is, their anger couldn't stop Mom and Dad. Nothing could have. Mom told me God himself couldn't have stopped her. When she met my dad she was done. She knew right away he was the one for her. She never looked back. Mallie claims a lot of things are God things, but that is the original God thing. If the first Mallie, my Aunt Tess' childhood friend, hadn't reached out to her and my mom and invited them to church, they wouldn't have learned to see beyond skin color. Those first few trips to church changed our whole family. They derailed the path Mom and Aunt Tess were on. Mom wouldn't have met Dad. Aunt Tess probably wouldn't have met Uncle Jonah. A God thing started my family."

"Why'd you tell me all this, Will?" I ate some of my own potato casserole, smiling when I realized Will was right. It was beyond good. Definitely something I would be making again.

"So you'd understand why I was thanking God for you."

"You think we're a God thing? Meant to be? You don't even really know me, Will. We've been in each other's lives for less than six months."

"I do, though. You can't spend close to a year tracking someone down and not learn about them. I know you worked at the same homeless shelter you lived in down in New Orleans, cooking to feed everyone else who lived there. I know you worked two jobs in Detroit while living in a rundown rental with six other people and still spent all your free time volunteering at a dog shelter. I know about all the good things you've done as you've bounced across the country. I've talked to the people whose lives you touched. You may not have stuck around any one place for long, but the things you did stayed. You're a good, kind person. You love to bake and cook for people. You'll do

191

anything to save a homeless dog or cat or person. You've touched so many lives. While I followed your trail across the country I got a bit of a crush on you and when you came here and started doing the same things without even thinking of it... I started to fall for you."

"Shut up." I flushed and looked away. I was drowning in emotions. Drowning in what could only be happiness.

"Nope. I can't. I love you, Joy. Get used to hearing it because I'm going to spend the rest of our lives telling you."

I smiled and looked down at my plate. I was surprised to see most of my food was gone and glanced over and saw Will's plate was empty too.

"Time for desert," I announced, standing and carrying both our plates back to the kitchen.

"Joy..."

"Just hang on one second. Hold your thought. I made something special for you."

I pulled the little white cake box out from behind Will's toaster. I'd worried he'd spot it but it had stayed well hidden.

"You made me dessert, too?"

"I made us dessert." I took my time getting the cake box, wanting to say my peace first. "You see. I realized something recently. It doesn't really matter that you don't know much about me and that I don't know much about you."

I smiled and set the cake in front of him, lifting off the lid with a flourish. "Like I said, the cake is for us. The message on the cake is for you though."

Watching him read the message I'd piped on the little cake was an experience. First, he was happy because there was cake. The man had a serious sweet tooth. Next he was surprised there was a message on the cake. As he took in the three words I'd piped on the snowy white icing something beyond happiness took over.

"Are you serious?" he asked, looking up at me. "You love me?"

"Yeah. Turns out, I agree. It is a God thing. We are meant to be. I love you and I'm pretty sure I never stood a chance."

He jumped out of his chair so fast he knocked it over, making me jump. He caught me around the waist pulling me to him and planting a quick kiss on my lips.

"How about some cake," I said as he stepped back, still grinning at me like a fool. I knew my face matched his though. I could feel the happiness in every part of me.

"Wait, wait," he dashed over to his forgotten suit jacket and pulled his cell phone out. "We'll want to show our kids this one day."

I burst out laughing when he took a picture of the message on the cake. I'd done the same thing before I put it in the box and I'd said the same thing to myself. *Someday I'll want to show this to our kids.*

Chapter Forty-One

Six months later...

I had worked my way through my to-do list from the bottom up. Will proposed to me on the night I told him I loved him. Then again two days later. Then a week later. I told him he had to wait until I got to it. I had a long list, after all. I had to take my time and make sure I got to everything.

The first thing I tackled was making peace with Lane. Like Walter had said, she had missed several days of work after he'd told her. I gave her until Friday, then I tracked her down. Finding her had been easy as pie. As it turned out, she lived just across the square and down a few blocks in a house with several friends. She hadn't wanted to talk to me but I'd camped out on her front porch until nearly ten that night. I waited her out just as my mom had done to me months earlier. It had worn her down and she'd invited me in. We'd talked until the next morning. Talked about everything -- movies, music, boys, school, and what it meant now that we knew each other as sisters. Lane had come to work the next day, though, so I felt victorious. It had taken a while but we were building something. It helped that we had already become friends before the news of our shared father had thrown a kink in things.

The next thing I'd taken on was hiring more help at the bakery. Mallie's wedding cake had really put us on the map and we'd been slammed from almost the minute after the wedding. I'd gotten lucky when Gia had come in and applied. She was a single mom with a teenage boy and needed the work. She was also a great baking assistant. As an added bonus, Gia and Mom hit it off right away and became fast friends.

After getting things running better at the bakery I stressed Will out a bit more and added a few things to my to-do list. I enlisted Isabel's help and together we recreated a bunch of vintage baking ads on big boards we'd liberated from Mallie's stash of scrap wood. The artwork had been just what the bakery had been missing. With the walls dressed up it finally felt like my place.

While I was putting off Will's repeated proposals, I worked on things with my father, slowly growing a relationship with him and slowly forgiving him. Mom worked on the same thing and I started to see the spark between them that had once existed. The connection was still there. I was excited to watch and see what would happen between them.

I said yes to Will when he made it a baker's dozen of proposals. That had felt like enough and thirteen had always been one of my favorite numbers. Life accelerated once we got engaged. Everything just flashed by until it was almost the big day. Then I realized there was one more thing I wanted to do. One thing I'd left off my to-do list. So I'd reached out to an old friend. I'd found Carson in Alaska. It had been a lucky guess. He had a list of one hundred trails he wanted to backpack. I had remembered several were ones he'd wanted to hike in the spring in Alaska. I got lucky and caught him in Denali National Park. He'd just returned from a day hike and had his cell phone turned on for once. We'd talked for hours, getting caught back up on each other's lives. He hadn't made the wedding but he said he'd be down to see me soon.

I refocused on the present and pulled up my to-do list on my phone, smiling at the list. Just one thing left. *Marry Will.* I swiped right, drawing a line through it. *All done*, I thought. I sighed and yawned, stretching out in the bed. Beside me Will stirred in his sleep.

"Husband," I whispered and he slept on, oblivious. Two days into our honeymoon and I was up at five in the morning. Again. My brain was just hard wired to rise before the sun. I slipped out of bed without waking him, wrapped up in the fluffy white hotel robe, and stole his laptop from the nightstand. If he could work while we were supposed to be vacationing I could at least check my email and my social media.

I logged on and found a surprise. An email from our wedding photographer. I was shocked she'd already edited the photos. I followed the link and slipped two days back in time. While Will slept, I relived our wedding day. There were pictures of me getting ready, Mom doing my hair, Lane sitting nearby laughing. There were several of me in my dress. I'd worn vintage just like Mallie had, only I'd gone for something from the 1970s. The dress had been a mess when Lane and I found it at a vintage shop in Lubbock. The lace stained from age. It was floor length and swallowed me. As it turned out, my sister was as good on a sewing machine as I was. We shortened it up to my knees and dyed it a pale, icy blue transforming it. The pictures of it made me smile. I wasn't going to box up the dress. Lane and I had already planned to dye it again and turn it into a fun cocktail dress.

I clicked my way through picture after picture seeing Will and Jackson getting ready, our fathers talking, our mothers laughing. It had snowed that day and we'd been able to take photos in the carpet of white before the late April sunshine had melted it away. The photos continued, documenting every moment. Saying our vows. Our first kiss as husband and wife. Walking back down the long center aisle of the Rio Verde Baptist church. Cutting the wedding cake -- my own creation covered entirely in rainbow sprinkles. Dancing with each other, then our parents, then each other's parents. Me dancing with Jackson's son Taylor. Laughing guests. Playful kids. Even one at the very end taken a few days before the wedding -- myself with BC in the bakery. I couldn't take my best feline friend to the wedding but I'd wanted him included somehow. He'd been the first friend I'd made in Rio Verde, after all.

It was hard to believe it had all happened just two days ago. It was even more difficult to believe it had been less than a year since I'd come to Rio Verde trying to figure out why I suddenly owned a bakery. I'd said it over and over but it would always be true. I was amazed at how much things had changed in my world in so short a time.

As I sat at the computer, another email popped in. This one was from my mom. It just had a picture attached and a note. *I thought you'd want to save this with your wedding photos, Joy-bear.* I opened the picture and smiled. It was one of me again. This time though it was just a cell phone shot instead of a fancy professional photo. It meant more than any of the others though. It showed my now father-in-law baptizing me at the church. I'd wanted to dedicate my life to the Lord before I married Will so Noah gave me a quick ceremony the night before the wedding. Just Will and I and our parents. I hadn't wanted to make a big deal about it. It had been a big deal to me though. All those God things Mallie had talked about. I could see now how all the apparently random things had really been moments that led me to the place I was meant to be. All those years of not paying God any attention and He'd been quietly guiding me down the right path the whole time.

Epilogue

After the honeymoon...

The muffled buzz of my alarm woke me. Stretching, I opened one eye then the next, staring up at the familiar dark ceiling of home. Home. I was home. I reached under my pillow and canceled the alarm, looking over at the sleeping form beside me.

"Still asleep," I whispered. It had been just over a week and I learned one very important thing. My husband was a hard sleeper. It was going to serve him well being married to an early rising baker.

I slipped out of bed and paused, looking back at him. I still couldn't stop smiling when I thought about it. I hadn't come back to Rio Verde looking for love but I'd been lucky and found it. I'd found so much more in fact. A family. Faith. Things I couldn't even name. This special little town had changed my life.

I tiptoed across the room and into the bathroom. I had to go start the day's baking. There was no reason to get him up at the insanely early time of five o'clock. Insane to him at least. It was my normal.

I was dressed and downstairs quickly, turning on the lights in the kitchen before opening up the loading dock door. It was Tuesday, which meant my delivery of eggs and milk would be here soon. I unlocked the side door next, knowing Mom would be over in a bit to fire up the ovens. She'd moved into Will's house while we were gone. We still had to figure out where we were going to live but were trying out the bakery apartment first. Mom was being supportive, willingly moving out to give us space to figure out the whole being married thing.

I unlocked the front door next, knowing Lane would come in that way. She'd walk over before long. She had helped Mom run the place while Will and I were gone. She'd turned out to be a great baker. I didn't know what I'd do without her. She'd also turned out to be totally good with a surprise big sister. I was excited to see her. I'd missed my little sis while we were gone.

Gia wouldn't be in until her son was off to school for the day. She was a new fixture in my world but I was excited to see her again, too. We'd had so much fun on our honeymoon down on the Texas Gulf Coast, but coming home and getting back to our real lives was better. It was where we both wanted to be.

I returned to the kitchen and flipped on the radio, turning it from a Christian station to a local news station. I wanted to get caught up on my town while I baked. We'd been home less than a day and felt like I had missed tons of the Rio Verde news and gossip.

"Overnight, we learned the name of the Good Samaritan involved in yesterday's robbery at Fancy's Truck Stop. Rio Verde mechanic Mateo Baca was shot during the incident. Witnesses stated that Baca was shot when one of the suspects aimed his gun at one of the witnesses. Baca and an off-duty state trooper attempted to protect the witness and Baca was shot in the struggle and airlifted to a hospital in Lubbock. The two suspects are both in custody and facing a laundry list of charges. State law enforcement has informed us that the two men are thought to have been responsible for the string of robberies that have plagued the area for almost a year. The station extends our prayers to Baca's family. A fund has been set up at the Rio Verde bank in Baca's name to help his family cover medical expenses."

Mom appeared in the doorway of the kitchen as the newscast ended. Her face was a mix of sadness and concern that I'm sure mirrored my own.

"Oh... no. Not Teo."

"I was hoping I'd get here before you heard it on the radio. I've been at the hospital all night with Luz and everyone else."

I put my hand to my face, covering my mouth, trying to hold on and keep control of my emotions. Wordlessly, she stepped over and wrapped me in a hug.

"I've already called Lane. She'll be here in a few minutes and will open the shop. There is enough stuff already baked. She and Gia can handle it by themselves for a day. Unless you just want to close up."

I stepped out of her embrace, turning toward the loading dock as the beeping of a truck drew my attention. Suddenly nothing else mattered. Not the bakery. Not the delivery. Not opening up and seeing customers. I just needed to go upstairs and wake up Will. And we needed to get in the car and go to our friends.

"Are there any orders to get out?"

Mom nodded and told me about the orders for birthday cakes needing to be delivered that day.

"Okay. Call Lane and tell her to get those out and then close up shop. Family emergency. I'll take care of the delivery. Then go and get Will. We need to be with Luz more than we need to be working today."

Bonus Content

Recipes

Most of what Joy whips up in Abbott Bakery is based on real bits of yummy goodness I've either baked or eaten over the years. I can't take credit for Mallie's wedding cake though. That is inspired by the lavender lemon cookies from The Slice of Life Bakery in Palisade Colorado. So are Joy's stuffed rolls – the bakery makes jalapeno, ham, and cheese ones that are to die for. The personality of Abbott Bakery was inspired by this bakery as well. It's my favorite place in my favorite Colorado town. If you're ever in that part of the world, stop in. You won't be sorry.

Below are some of my own recipes that made it into Joy's bakery. I hope you'll try them. And enjoy them.

Elise

Oatmeal Flaxseed Chocolate Chip Cookies

3/4 cup all-purpose flour
3/4 cup whole wheat flour
1 cup oats
1/4 cup ground flaxseed
1 teaspoon baking soda
1/2 teaspoon cinnamon
6 tablespoons butter
6 tablespoons applesauce
1 cup organic sugar
3/4 cup packed brown sugar
2 eggs
1 teaspoon vanilla extract
1 cup dark chocolate chips

Mix the dry ingredients in a medium bowl and set aside.
Beat the butter and sugars until fluffy.
Beat in the eggs and vanilla.

Slowly add roughly half of the flour mixture, then add the chocolate chips, and then the rest of the flour. Spoon out dough onto parchment lined backing sheets and bake at 350 degrees for 11 minutes.

(These are also super yummy with a cup of freeze-dried strawberries.)

Pumpkin Cookies with Nutella

2-1/2 cups all-purpose flour
1 teaspoon baking powder
1 teaspoon baking soda
3 teaspoons pumpkin pie spice
1/2 cup butter
1 cup sugar
1/2 cup brown sugar
1 can pumpkin puree
1 egg
1 teaspoon vanilla extract
1 13oz container of Nutella

Combine dry ingredients in a medium bowl and set aside.
Cream butter and sugars.
Add pumpkin, egg, and vanilla and mix until smooth.
Blend in dry ingredients.
Scoop onto parchment lined baking sheets.
In a microwave safe container place a generous amount of Nutella and microwave until melted.
Place a small dollop of Nutella on each of the cookies and swirl in with a toothpick (or finger).
Bake at 350 degrees for 15-18 minutes.

Note: Cookies may be slightly sticky even when cool. Lightly dust them with powdered sugar to solve this.

Also, if you don't like Nutella, these are also amazing with butterscotch chips (1 cup). Or skip the chips and instead frost them with a cinnamon cream cheese frosting. (Recipe is below.)

Cinnamon Cream Cheese Frosting
1 package cream cheese (softened)
3 cups powdered sugar
1 tablespoon cinnamon
1 teaspoon vanilla
1/2 cup butter

Beat butter and cream cheese together.
Mix in powdered sugar.
Mix in vanilla and cinnamon.
Let frosting rest a bit before using. Can be stored in the fridge/freezer for a good while so its easy to make up in advance.

About the Author

A few years ago, a chance visit to a new church changed the path of Elise Phillips' life. After many years away from the church, Elise found her way back to the Lord. With the support of her friends, family, and church, finally she chased her writing dream. First, by getting a master's degree in Creative Writing from Southern New Hampshire University. Second, by turning her thesis project into a novel. Elise firmly believes that your talent is your gift from God and what you do with it is your gift to Him. Though currently working as a graphic designer, Elise hopes to one day be able to fully dedicate her life to writing stories filled with faith and God's love. In her spare time Elise tries to find time to pursue her many hobbies including photography, knitting, and above all else reading.

A fifth generation Texan, Elise calls the top of Texas home, residing in of Amarillo with her fur kids, Ice and CC. Elise is excited for the new adventures that writing is bringing into her life and can't wait to see what will come next

www.ingramcontent.com/pod-product-compliance
Lightning Source LLC
Chambersburg PA
CBHW020412210626
46816CB00006BB/2239